Annie O'Neil spent most of her childhood with her leg draped over the family rocking chair and a book in her hand. Novels, baking, and writing too much teenage angst poetry ate up most of her youth. Now Annie splits her time between corralling her husband into helping her with their cows, baking, reading, barrel racing (not really!) and spending some very happy hours at her computer, writing.

Also by Annie O'Neil

Tempted by Her Single Dad Boss
The Doctor's Marriage for a Month
A Return, a Reunion, a Wedding
Making Christmas Special Again
Risking Her Heart on the Single Dad
The Vet's Secret Son
Christmas Under the Northern Lights
A Family Made in Rome

The Island Clinic collection

The Princess and the Paediatrician

Discover more at millsandboon.co.uk.

HAWAIIAN MEDIC TO RESCUE HIS HEART

ANNIE O'NEIL

MILLS & BOON

First published in Great Britain 2021
by Mills & Boon, an imprint of HarperCollins*Publishers* Ltd,
1 London Bridge Street, London, SE1 9GF

www.harpercollins.co.uk

HarperCollins*Publishers*
1st Floor, Watermarque Building,
Ringsend Road, Dublin 4, Ireland

Large Print edition 2022

Hawaiian Medic to Rescue His Heart © 2021 Annie O'Neil

ISBN: 978-0-263-29366-1

02/22

To my Hawaiian Hero

CHAPTER ONE

"HAILANA'S IS THE BEST—now zip it!"

Lulu ran her fingers along her mouth, then made the *shaka* sign with her hand, the more peaceful gesture finally managing to silence her colleagues, who were coming near to blows over who knew the best "secret" place to buy garlic shrimp farther up the coast.

Ono grinds—the Hawaiian version of choice fast food outlets—were often the main topic of discussion, when the crew members weren't re-telling stories of recent rescues or actually res-cuing someone. Which, to be fair, was most of the time. But the tourist season was coming to an end and there was an extra splash of "sitting-around time," during which conversation usually revolved around food.

Lulu had five big brothers—each and every one of them born and bred right here on Oahu—so if anyone knew where the best garlic shrimp were, she did. Besides, she was acting crew chief, and there was an all-island alert sounding on the emergency scanner. Perfect shrimp on a cloud of beautifully steamed rice with an unctuous lashing of teriyaki sauce would have to wait.

She pointed to the dispatch radio on the counter. "Listen."

The voice on the radio crackled though again. "Family of four out on Mokoli'i."

The jocular banter fell to an abrupt halt as they listened to the rest of the report. Mom and dad... Two little boys... Thought they'd walk out to Mokoli'i, a tiny little island just under five hundred meters off the coast. The islet featured a couple of sea caves, two small idyllic beaches and, more to the point, no human population. People loved going out there for a taste of "desert island life." It was perfect...unless you didn't know when the tide came in.

This family had headed out toward the end of low tide, with a warning from the local lifeguards to come straight back. Because once the tide came in, walking back wasn't an option. The hotel they'd been staying in on the North Shore had been expecting them back for a dinner reservation an hour earlier, and there'd been no sign of them.

As a lifelong surfer, Lulu didn't need to be told there was no way they would be getting back without a boat. She knew the tidal schedule as well as she knew the menu at her local burger shack. And she ate out a lot. With the sun beginning its descent, and the tide only set to draw in higher, there was no time to waste.

Lulu swept the zipper round the first aid backpack she'd been restocking and shouldered it. "Casey, can you grab four life vests? Two adult, two children."

"Who wants to bet that they're *haoles*?" said Stewart, their helicopter pilot and sometimes speedboat captain, as he pulled on his Oahu Search and Rescue high-vis vest.

"What? You mean like you, mainlander?" ribbed Casey, her hair and make-up immaculate as ever as she shouldered her own first aid backpack, then howled in an imitation of how the Hawaiian word for foreigners was pronounced.

Casey howled a lot around Stew. The platinum-blonde medic and rescue staffer had been hired the same week as Lulu, and though they couldn't look more different—a tall, willowy funster against Lulu's petite surfer-girl vibe—

their core values were identical and they'd become instant friends.

Stewart threw up his hands and groaned. "Oh, c'mon, y'all! I've lived on the island forty years already! Surely that makes me a local."

"Not if you're still saying y'all," the rest of the team chorused as one.

Stew shook his head and grumbled something about islanders being stuck in their ways. Born in Texas, he'd used to try to shoot down their ribbing by insisting that Hawaii was his spiritual home. He'd moved here as soon as he'd been old enough to earn the airfare. Now, at sixty-three, he'd lived on the island long enough to learn the lingo, sport a teak-colored tan, and call all visitors to the islands foreigners—but not long enough to be considered a local.

Deep down, he knew the truth. You weren't Hawaiian unless you *were* Hawaiian. And his heart pumped Texas blood.

"Heads up." Lulu threw Stew the keys to the speedboat.

It was a small counterbalance for the regular ribbing he received. All the *You'll never be one of us* jibes had to be evened out by equal measures of appreciation. A crucial lesson being the youngest of six had taught her. It was all well and good to know where there was room for improvement—something her brothers regularly reminded her of—but it was equally important to be reminded that you were appreciated.

It was something she was still trying to teach them. She knew they loved her. Even if sometimes she had to dig incredibly deep beneath their insane overprotectiveness to see their love and respect—especially when it came across as claustrophobic and they seemed intent on never, *ever* letting her have a love life. But…whatever. If a prospective beau didn't want her enough to stand up to her brothers' *Don't you dare hurt my little sister* talks, she wasn't interested.

Not that a boyfriend was on her to-do list. Proving to their new boss—whoever he was— that she was top of her game was. And, more to the point, that she should've been given his job.

When their last crew chief—a cranky, sexist, would-rather-be-in-a-hammock-than-out-on-a-job boss—had retired a few weeks back, and Lulu had been made acting crew chief, she'd seen it as her personal mission to make every member of the crew feel appreciated. Worthy.

They were a small, motley, mismatched crew,

and in the three years since she'd joined the team hundreds of lives had been saved because of them. Today was her last day as acting chief, and she wanted to make sure they all knew how much she appreciated their support of her leadership. Even if she might not have dotted every *i* or crossed every *t*.

Stew caught the keys and gave her a grateful nod. "Thanks, peanut."

"That's boss lady peanut to you, mister." She grinned, arcing her arm in a gesture for the others to follow her to the dock.

"Ticktock, time's running out on that." Casey grimaced, jogging up alongside Lulu. "How're you doing with that? Preparing for the new boss?"

Lulu pulled a face. Not particularly well. She'd had all sorts of plans about having everything in such amazing shape that he would immediately see she should have been given the job and fly back to wherever he'd come from. But…time. There was never enough of it. Especially when her choices were rescuing people or paperwork. Eating or paperwork. And surfing or paperwork.

She wanted the job, but in her more honest, private moments she had her doubts. The predominantly desk-based work that defined the senior position wasn't really her thing. Now, if the job came with a PA, whose sole responsibility was filling in the endless forms so she herself could go out on all the rescues...

She pursed her lips. Even the bump in pay these past few weeks hadn't inspired her to get the piles of paperwork done. Which did beg the question: Did she really want it? Or was she happy as she was?

Having just one job instead of the two she was currently juggling would be nice. Although her job as a paramedic did go hand in hand with her search and rescue job. With the complementary training each job had, she knew she always had a bit of an edge when it came to making critical life-and-death decisions, and choosing overtime over a social life meant her savings account was getting incredibly close to the magic number she needed to put down a deposit on the dream house she had practically moved into already.

Turtle Hideaway.

The small property she'd been coveting for almost two years now was a traditional Hawaiian beach house, tucked into a small, miraculously private cove. Living there would mean access to some gentle surf, some lazy morning swims with sea turtles, an insanely beautiful view of the sunrise and, like the cherry on top of a perfect ice cream sundae, it was on the opposite side of the island from her big brothers.

All except for Laird, of course, who was on the Big Island studying his precious volcanoes.

Her parents had totally messed up, naming him after a surfer. She smiled at that thought. But her smile faded away before it had a chance to gain purchase.

Her parents hadn't lived long enough to know that he'd become a respected volcanologist. They hadn't lived long enough to know what any of them had become.

The radio squawked again, pulling her back into the moment.

"C'mon everyone. Wheels up and motor in the water!"

She tried and failed to stuff her trademark braid under her Oahu Search and Rescue cap. Hair down to your butt tended to have a mind of its own. Sure, she could cut it, but…she wasn't the *complete* tomboy her brothers accused her of being.

Giving up, she flicked it back into its usual

position, down the line of her spine, and announced, "Let's go get these goofballs."

"You coming?" Stewart feigned surprise.

Lulu hesitated, knowing her remit was to stay back and man the radios at HQ. But it was her last day. Surely one itty-bitty rescue wouldn't hurt?

Casey glanced at her phone, then made an *uh-oh* noise.

"What?"

"The dispatch has also gone to the OST."

Lulu's full lips thinned. Their "rivals"—the Ocean Safety Team. Headed by none other than her brother Makoa—aka the Mak Attack. The one man on the island who knew each callout he took meant taking his little sister out of the ocean. It was a favorite pastime of his. Which was precisely why they needed to get a move on.

"We're closest," she said, picking up her pace.

It wasn't strictly a lie. They were almost equidistant, with an edge of maybe a kilometer or so. But her brother's crew had bigger boats, with larger engines, and a huge team waiting dockside for just this type of rescue. It shouldn't be a competition, but thanks to her brothers' nonstop campaign to get her to commit to a desk job, so nothing ever happened to her like—

She stopped the memory short. Hanging on to the darkest day of their lives would never bring their parents back.

Fifteen minutes and one hair-raising boat ride later, Lulu and her team pulled up to the tiny island where the family were backed up against a rock precipice, madly waving their arms except for the father, who was holding one of the little boys in his. They all looked terrified.

Any thoughts of shooting up a victorious flare gun to show her brother they'd "won" the race disappeared. This family needed help.

Lulu pulled off her regulation top so that she was only wearing her favorite long-sleeved short wetsuit and an ankle-height pair of ocean boots. The sea urchins round here were notorious.

Without waiting for the boat to fully come to a halt, she jumped into the waist-height water, backpack on, and waded to shore, pushed on by the rising tide while the rest of her crew secured the boat in the shallows.

"Please! Help our boy!" The tearstained mother cried, pointing to the dark-haired little boy cradled in his father's arms. "Jamie stepped on something spiky and we couldn't get it out. He refused to head back to the island before the tide came in and…and—"

The distraught woman released a sob of relief, then began to pour out an incredibly detailed story of how the day had begun and how they had ended up here, while Lulu focused her attention where it needed to be. On the boy.

One quick examination revealed that, yes, he'd stepped on a spiny sea urchin. The long spines could really sting, and it looked as though Jamie had stepped on not just one, but several of the spiky sea creatures—and with both of his feet. The odd puncture wound was generally easily rectified with a pair of tweezers, after a good old foot soak, but one glance at the boy's pallor and a quick tally of the black and blue puncture wounds told Lulu he would very likely need a course of antibiotics.

"How long have you been out here?"

The husband and wife exchanged a look. "Three hours? Maybe four?"

The husband shook his head and said he'd left his watch back at the hotel, wanting to really enjoy the last day of vacation with his family without worrying about the time. "I don't get much time with the kids when we're back home, see? So I told them—Jamie? Robbie? We're going to have a one hundred percent family day."

"Well, you got that, all right," Lulu said, her full lips narrowing into a wince. "And with a bit more drama than you anticipated."

Lulu got the father to lay Jamie down on the ever-decreasing beach while she examined his feet. "Are they stinging?" she asked him.

He nodded, tears beading in his eyes. Despite wanting to read the riot act to the family, for not checking the tide tables, her heart did go out to them. They'd been doing what families were meant to do—sticking with one another.

"Tell me, Jamie, how are your muscles feeling? Strong or weak?" She struck a muscle pose, then let herself wilt in a comedic flop. As she'd hoped, the little boy smiled and tried to make a muscle pose. Okay. So he was a bit weak. But he'd been scared for a few hours and those stings hurt without any sort of topical antibiotic or hydrocortisone cream.

She held her hand close to his feet, not touching the arch, where the concentration of spines was the heaviest. They were swollen and, yes, there was some heat radiating from them. At least no one had tried to pull the spines out by hand. They'd need a good soak in warm water and—her mother's home remedy—a healthy splash of vinegar.

The reminder of her mother gave her heart another short, sharp twist. She forced herself to re-form the pain into pride.

Her mother would have loved knowing Lulu was using her remedies. Loved it that her daughter hadn't shied away from the career she'd always wanted, despite both of her parents' lives being cut so short in a similar one.

Logging the thought and shelving it, Lulu pulled out a temperature gun and held it to Jamie's forehead. "Hands up!" she commanded playfully.

Once again, the little boy did try to play along as she took his temperature. It was up by a degree. Nothing serious, but something to keep an eye on. It was also a reason not to apply hydrocortisone cream straight away. That course of antibiotics was looking more and more likely.

"Is he going to have to go to the hospital?" asked the boy's father. "Our flights are first thing tomorrow morning, and if he needs extensive treatment I'm going to have to talk to the airlines. I heard you're meant to, you know..." the father lowered his voice "...urinate on the injury."

Lulu wrinkled her nose. "Luckily, that's a myth."

"Of course." He gave a nervous laugh. "I knew that. I was just confirming it for my wife."

His wife threw him a chastening look.

"Hey, chief!" Casey called from the side of the boat, where she was standing at the ready. "Need a stretcher?"

Lulu eyed the water depth, ever-increasing. Her very tall brother could have carried the boy. With one hand. All of her brothers could. It was like being related to five Jason Momoas or The Rocks. Tattoos... Muscles to spare... And more than enough attitude to circle the entire island group.

They constantly teased Lulu for her diminutive stature, insisting she'd been adopted because of her much smaller frame—which had, early on, earned her the nickname Mini-Menehune. She didn't know how many times she'd bellowed at them to take it back, telling them that, at five foot two, she was volumes taller than the island's mythical dwarves. Besides, she didn't have magical powers. If she did they'd know all about it.

These days when they Mini-Menehune'd her she just rolled her eyes. She'd made her stature work for her the same way they'd made theirs work for them. No one was better in an earthquake or collapse rescues than she was.

Boo-yah!

"A stretcher would be great," she said, and Casey began climbing over the edge of the boat with one.

They both knew the family's safety was more important than pride. They quickly transferred Jamie, then Robbie, and then the parents. Another quick boat ride and they were back at the OSR dock. A man they didn't recognize was waiting on the dock with a wheelchair.

The closer they got, the more Lulu's spine pulled up to attention. He was looking out at them with an unsmiling face. That wasn't what had her attention, though.

He was drop-dead gorgeous.

Frowning possibly made him even sexier. He was tall. Not as tall as her brothers, but he definitely would clock in at six foot something. Athletic... The lean variety as opposed to her brothers' bodybuilder aesthetic. Amazing blue eyes that could easily put a girl in a trance.

Cheekbones begging for some fingertips to run the length of them. Chestnut-colored hair... Not sun-kissed... So a *haole*. A *haole* wearing an OSR jacket.

A wash of horror swept through her.

The grumpy hottie was the new boss.

She knew he was coming. Had known it for weeks. They all had. But...kind of like the mythical dwarves...she'd never entirely, actually believed he would come.

She forced on a smile and waved. *"Aloha!"*

Ew! That had been high-pitched. She didn't dare look at the rest of the crew, because she could feel them staring at her with *What kind of weird voice was that?* in their eyes.

He did that chin-lift thing guys did when they chose actions over words and didn't answer—which was rude. His eyes narrowed as if inspecting her for flaws.

A weird urge to rattle them all off for him seized her. She wasn't in regulation uniform. They shouldn't have taken this call. They should've left someone back at base. They should've locked the office. She should've done the towering pile of paperwork sitting in the in tray.

There were also the more personal flaws. Her

hair was probably mental. She chose gut reactions against by-the-book reactions. She hated peas. Probably could've eaten more vegetables in general. And there was always room for improvement in her flossing routine.

Bah!

Woulda...shoulda...coulda...

They'd saved this family from drowning. That was what mattered.

So she kept her smile bright, and waited for a response to her cheery island greeting other than a frown.

His bright sapphire-blue eyes scanned her, then flashed with an unchecked hit of warning when their eyes met. She fought the tiniest of trembles and turned it into a careless shrug. Their dueling *I see you* stares changed into something else. Something every bit as heated but...different. Like butterflies in her stomach. That kind of different.

Which was entirely unprofessional and made any *I'm right, you're wrong* posturing completely evaporate along with her high-pitched *aloha*.

She couldn't have the hots for him. No way.

Not for a *haole*. Not for someone who was this

frowny and bereft of manners. And definitely not for a boss who had yet to say hello.

Hmmph.

From the thinning of his irritatingly sensual mouth, it was looking like *someone* needed a little lesson on island greetings.

She jumped onto the dock the second they pulled up and gave him a jaunty salute. Maybe he was ex-military, like their last chief.

He didn't salute back.

Okay. Whatever. She still wasn't going to let his whole stoic *I can play statues better than you can* thing unnerve her. Unlike the last boss man, this one was going to know that Lulu Kahale was a force to be reckoned with.

"Aloha," she said again, lifting her hand into the *shaka* sign. "Lulu Kahale. Acting crew chief at your service."

"Zach Murphy," he said, without returning the *shaka*. "You're grounded. I'll take over from here."

CHAPTER TWO

ZACH MIGHT AS well have pressed an "erupt" button on the island's volcanoes for all the tension there was in the air. Or maybe it was the tropical heat he was pretty sure he'd never get used to. Either way, he was uncomfortable.

Hell.

He'd wanted to make an impression when he arrived here at the station. A bad one, however, had not been the goal. And this one was about as bad as it got.

Before he'd even met her, Lulu Kahale had managed to crawl right under his skin. Which took some doing. Now that he had met her, he knew his instincts had been spot-on.

Beautiful. Proud. Brimming with unchecked energy. She was a force of nature. More hurricane than rainbow at this exact moment. Although even that barely disguised sneer of hers didn't detract from her striking aesthetic. It might even be illuminating it.

Pitch-black hair he bet mimicked an oil slick when it was fanned out on a pillow. Liquid eyes that looked like molten gold. Lips so full and soft that a dangerous image of what they'd look like bruised from kisses temporarily blinded him.

He rubbed his thumbs in his eyes, refocused his brain and forced himself to pour the energy she was pulling from him back into the task at hand.

Even so, as he took the boy from one of the crew's arms and placed him in the wheelchair, Zach was giving himself invisible punches in the face.

His parents had warned him. *Hawaiians do things differently. There's another way of getting things done out here.* And, more pressingly, *Don't expect things to run by the same book they did back in New York.*

They'd got that right.

Rescue crews were extraordinary people. They willingly dove headfirst into scenarios most humans were genetically programmed to flee. Dangerous ones. Fires. Floods. Cliff edges. The whole damn ocean. They didn't deserve coddling, but they certainly deserved respect.

That ethos had been the key to managing the

fire rescue medical teams he'd helmed back in New York. Gratitude combined with one crystal-clear edict: no bending the rules. *Ever.*

Which was precisely why the team behind Oahu Search and Rescue had brought him on board. According to the management, this team needed "a bit more starch in their collars."

They weren't part of Hawaii's famous Ocean Safety Team. This crew was more...off radar. They went a step beyond. Took the rescues the OST weren't trained for. Belayed into the steepest ravines to find hikers who'd lost their way. Dove out of helicopters into a stormy ocean to find surfers sucked out to sea by the powerful currents. And countless other scenarios. In short, they risked life and limb to save other people's.

His new bosses, based back on the mainland, had drilled a second message into him when granting his three-month mandatory probation. One that had been ringing in his head from the moment he'd accepted the job. Funding for Oahu Search and Rescue would only continue if everything was shipshape. From what he'd seen so far, it most assuredly wasn't.

He needed this job. He needed it as much as he needed the heart that beat in his chest. The

heart that beat in his son's. They were both bat-
tered and bruised and they were relying on this
new start more than he could put into words.
So, yeah...

When he'd arrived at the office and found no
one there, the door wide open and an overflow-
ing tray of weeks-old paperwork, then eagle-eyed
the crew returning, half in regulation gear, half
very definitely not, he'd seen red. They weren't
just compromising his professional future with
this slapdash approach. They were compromising everyone's health and safety. And that was
unacceptable.

If this had officially been his first day, he'd
have been halfway through reading this woman
the riot act. This... Lulu.

For the first time ever he felt as if his perfectly
appropriate anger was hobbled.

Shouting at Lulu would feel like shouting at a
happy-go-lucky puppy. Between his gut and the
vibes she was arrowing straight at his jugular,
he knew shouting would only turn things from
bad to worse.

One eyebrow lifted in an imperious arc, she
shifted from one hip to the other, droplets of
water glistening on the high-cut arch of her wet-

suit where her hip met her thigh. Caramel-colored thighs that should very definitely be hidden behind regulation board shorts or a knee-length wetsuit. Not this…this body-hugging short wetsuit that swept up and along her curves to her heart-shaped face.

Those flame-licked amber eyes were unblinking as she maintained her gaze on him, pulled some lip balm from who knew where and swept it along first her upper lip, then her lower, as if preparing for battle.

He felt as if they were speaking to him. Her lips. Begging him to kiss the disdain away. Turn it into something sweeter.

Or maybe the heat had officially sent him tropical.

He threw some imaginary cold water on his head.

He'd thought he was immune to "drop-dead gorgeous" after things with his wife had gone so spectacularly wrong, but no. This woman's beauty was something else altogether. Natural. Spirited. Every bit as heated as the lava threatening to make a show over on the Big Island.

As his eyes swept the length of her, hot licks of desire tugged at parts of him he'd rather not be dealing with right now. He saw her giving him the same once-over, with an expression that shifted from angry to impossible to read. One enemy sizing up the other? Or two people getting off on the wrong foot, then realizing seconds too late there was one hell of a mutual attraction?

He made a big mental X over the latter option and concentrated on the task at hand. Getting things back on track for a positive working relationship.

To keep the unwanted carnal sensations from making any visual impression, Zach pulled himself up to his full height and crossed his arms over his chest, hoping to draw Lulu's attention back to his face.

"So. What exactly does my being grounded entail?"

Lulu was staring him straight in the eye, clearly unintimidated by him physically or professionally.

"Are you sending me to my room? No dates for a month? No candy bars till Christmas?"

One of the crew behind her tried and failed to turn a snigger into a cough. This was Lulu's crowd, and he had five seconds to find a way not to be permanently branded The Bad Guy.

Zach shifted on his feet, transfixed by Lulu's amber-colored eyes that were flaring with coppery hits of indignation. He'd definitely made the wrong call. She wasn't belligerent—she was proud. She wasn't reckless—she was permanently poised for action. She wasn't trying to one-up him—she was trying to hang on to her hard-won rung on the ladder.

Not hard enough, though. He was the new chief, and as such there had to be some lines drawn in the sand.

"The patient's your priority for now," he said.

It was as much of an olive branch as he could give without throwing up his hands and conceding defeat.

"Oh? So you *do* want me to do my job, then?"

Lulu didn't bother double checking. She made a signal to her team that they should carry on what they were doing—which was, in fairness, their job. A blonde woman and two other men, all kitted out in regulation neon orange OSR shirts and board shorts, helped the rest of the family off the boat, while Lulu took command of the boy in the wheelchair.

One of the crew offered him a quick, apologetic, "Pretty sure she needs an extra set of hands…" in explanation as they hurried after Lulu, who was strutting down the dock as if she were a pop star who'd just swept the Grammys.

Whether her intent was to show off her curves or not was hard to tell, but suffice it to say she had it and she was flaunting it.

He couldn't help it. He grinned. Lulu was gutsy. He was going to have to match her point for point, then win some extra ones if he wanted to win the team's respect.

"Eh, bruh?" The man who had been piloting the speedboat clapped him on the shoulder. "I'm guessing you're the new boss man?"

Zach nodded.

He introduced himself as Stewart, rattled off a quick ream of credentials, then lowered his voice as he tilted his head toward Lulu, now disappearing into the clinic.

"She's all right—so cut her some slack, yeah? She's spent a lifetime proving to her five big brothers that she's just as tough as they are, so she tends to come on a bit strong at first."

Zach whistled. Five big brothers, eh?

There had been plenty of second-and-third-generation firemen at his station like that. Trying to prove they were just as good or better than those who had come before them. Hell… *He* was a bit like that.

Nothing like following in the wake of a father who had all but been the poster boy for the 9/11 rescue effort. Everyone on the fire crews had gone above and beyond, but his dad's rescue efforts had captured the press's attention. For a while. The fact that he'd had to take early retirement because of the battering his body had taken hadn't warranted so much as a column inch. No one had cared about pulmonary fibrosis in a fireman outside of his prime. They'd cared even less when he'd moved to Hawaii to try to give his lungs a break.

Anyway… He shook his head and focused on the problem at hand.

"Rules are the same for everyone," Zach said, almost by rote.

Stewart rocked back on his heels and made a noise that, once again, had Zach giving himself an invisible pop on the kisser. He was definitely walking an out-of-the-frying-pan-into-the-fire path today.

"Yeah, bruh… I see where you're going. But…" Stewart cleared his throat and gave his chin a scrub, obviously trying to put his words in an order he thought would penetrate Zach's thick skull. "The thing is… Lulu's got health and safety ingrained in her bones, you know? She's lived and breathed this stuff her entire life, but never been given proper recognition for it. The last boss…he tended to 'put Baby in the corner,' if you know what I mean."

Zach shook his head. No. He did not.

"You know…" Stewart opened his hands as if it was obvious. *"Dirty Dancing?"*

Another vision of those water droplets skidding along Lulu's bare thighs blinded Zach for a second. "Nope," he said.

"Not a film reference kind of guy?"

"I prefer facts to fiction," Zach said, knowing that the direction this conversation was headed wasn't endearing him to Stewart, who would inevitably report back to the rest of the crew. He put up a hand in an attempt to rescue the situation. "Look. I'm still a bit jet-lagged, and I probably shouldn't have rocked up barking orders in the middle of a rescue. I suspect we're all going to have to take a bit of time to get used to one another."

"Don't worry, man." Stewart gave him a congenial clap on the shoulder that made it very clear the man's age had done little to diminish his strength. "We all have false starts. The thing about Hawaii is..." He looked out to the sea, then up to the sun, then back to Zach. "We all come here seeking instant perfection, but the thing about paradise..."

He opened his eyes wide, actively inviting Zach to ask him to unveil the mysteries of Polynesia.

"What is the thing about paradise?" Zach asked, finally realizing that Stewart wasn't going to share his island wisdom until he was asked.

"You have to earn it." Stewart said tapping the side of his nose. *"Ho'oponopono."*

"Come again?"

Stewart repeated the word, then explained. "It's the Hawaiian practice of reconciliation and forgiveness. A way to free yourself from negative thoughts and feelings. Building a gateway to happiness and fulfilment of your dreams."

Zach looked at Stewart. Really looked at him. Beneath the tan and the laid-back stance he saw a man who'd fought and failed and fought again, until he'd truly won that aura of inner calm and—dare he say it?—control of his own destiny.

Another thing to take note of. Just because a person was relaxed and smiley didn't necessarily mean they flaunted the rules. They respected them. They just had their own way of paying said respect.

Son of a gun...

He couldn't believe that he, Zach "Read the Regs" Murphy, was even thinking this. But maybe every now and again seeing the rules from another angle was the better option.

After all, the divorce lawyers had recommended he and his son stay in New York, but in the end he'd gone with his gut. Harry's special needs could as easily be catered for in Hawaii as they had been in New York, but if he was going to continue working he needed help. The kind you only got from family.

His ex, Christina, had always prioritized her work over the two of them. It had been one of the first fault lines in their marriage. Her modeling career had meant she was rarely in New York, so in order to be close to family—*proper family*—he'd sought out a nine-to-five job that tapped into his skill base, moved to Hawaii, and bought a house not far from his parents' condo.

He'd seen his parents transformed by island

life, and was hoping that whatever was in the water out here would do the same for him and his son. The simple truth was that his parents had moved to Hawaii because they'd been hurting. Just like he was now. So, yeah. Like it or not, Zach needed some of this *ho'oponopono*. Big-time.

Stewart made the hand gesture Lulu had and said, "We good, boss?"

"Absolutely." Zach nodded, with a *Thanks for the insight* smile.

He watched him walk down the dock and disappear into the clinic, where a roar of laughter seemed to add an extra hit of color to the scene. Bright red plantation style building... White sand... Blue sky... Greener than green mountains soaring up in the background...

He decided to stay where he was. Absorb some of the atmosphere. After all, this was going to be where he worked and, to be fair, there were several highly trained emergency medical professionals in there with the boy and his family, who knew more about stepping on sea urchins than he did.

Not much call for sea urchin spine extraction in the heart of Manhattan.

About twenty minutes passed. Then the family left, the father carrying his little boy in his arms, white bandages round his feet, and the blonde woman—Casey, if he remembered correctly— walking with them to their car with a small sheaf of papers.

He gave a begrudging smile. Okay. They weren't so "off regulation" that they didn't give their patients the paperwork they'd need for their insurance and the doctors back home.

Before they got in the car, Casey put a fresh lei round the little boy's neck and called out a hearty *"Aloha!"* as they pulled away.

Zach leaned back on the rock he'd taken up residence on and let the sun hit him full on the face. It was a warm day, but not the kind of "city hot" Manhattan sometimes sweltered under. The air was a mix of sweet and salty. The breeze felt like silk. Even the birds seemed to ratchet their songs up a notch out here in the tropics.

"He *what*?"

Zach sat up. Definitely not a songbird's cry.

He looked round at the parking lot. The beach. The rescue HQ and—ah…there she was. Five feet and two inches of electricity and venom, heading straight toward him without so much as a trace of a smile on her face.

Lulu was wearing a pair of hip-hugging jeans and a long-sleeved T-shirt with the name of a security company on the front of it. The neck was ripped out so that it slipped off one of her shoulders as she stormed his way. She was also dragging an ominous black thunder cloud in her wake.

Zach felt the sand shift beneath his feet as he quite literally dug his heels in for whatever confrontation was about to come.

"Zach Murphy?" Lulu asked, her voice with a low, ominous tone.

"Yes?"

"I have a bone to pick with you."

He shrugged some fortitude into his bloodstream. It was better that they resolve whatever it was now rather than let things simmer.

"Fair enough." He closed the space between them, keeping his voice on the lighter side of neutral. "What's on your mind?"

"You bought my house."

CHAPTER THREE

ZACH GAVE LULU a double take—which, insanely, made her even angrier. There were the tiniest fractals of vulnerability piercing through the defensive stance he'd shifted into, and she didn't like thinking she'd put them there. She was angry. Sure. But she wasn't a bully.

Now she had to be angry with herself *and* him! *Jerk.* He really knew how to make a bad day worse.

His three-month probation was going to be exhausting if every day was like today. Particularly now that he'd bought a house. *Her* house. It meant he had no plans to fail the probation. No back-up plan in place back on the mainland. He was putting down roots. This was a man who planned to stay.

Zach Murphy scrubbed a hand through his regulation haircut, making it adorably messy. *Idiot.* He looked over his shoulders toward the sea, as if expecting a support team of combat mermaids to appear, and when that didn't happen he returned his gaze to her, the bright blueness of it knocking a lungful of air out of her for the second time today.

"I—sure. I bought a house. It was for sale. I have the paperwork and the mortgage to prove it."

He looked confused rather than confrontational—which, if she were in a reasonable mood, she knew was a pretty generous response. But in true Lulu style she had to finish what she'd started, and this little chat they were having wasn't about making nicey-nicey with the man who had not only bought her dream house but had also taken the job that would have enabled her to buy the house in question.

The fact that she didn't really want said job wasn't important now...

"The thing is," Lulu intoned, feeling the steam almost literally coming out of her ears, "Turtle Hideaway was *mine*." She poked herself in the chest with a bit more gusto than she probably should have.

Zach shook his head again, even more confused. "So...if you didn't want to sell it, why'd you put it on the market?"

"No!" Lulu threw up her hands, cross with herself for letting the conversation get so muddled. "I wanted to *buy* it and you beat me to it!"

"The Realtor didn't say anything about anyone else having put in an offer..."

Lulu barely stopped a low growl from roaring up and out of her throat. "I was *going* to put in an offer, but I needed a few more months to increase my deposit."

She bit down on the inside of her cheek. *Crud.* She hadn't meant to admit that.

Zach Murphy was an intelligent man. And talented. And married to all the rule books that had ever been written about anything ever.

Not that she'd ever admit it, but—*yes.* She'd totally looked him up on the internet just now, while Casey had picked sea urchin spines out of that poor little boy's feet. He had qualifications she couldn't imagine garnering. Emergency medicine clearly stoked his arterial fires.

His father had been a fire station medic during 9/11, in charge of multiple rescue crews and lauded as a hero by the press. His grandfather before him had actually *started* a fire station in a poor area of town where no one else would work. And Zach, in keeping with the family tradition, had led a junior firefighter youth group from the age of fourteen and had been the first to acquire all his first aid badges.

He'd risen through the New York City Fire Department ranks on his own merit rather than hanging on to the coattails of his forebears, and at last check had overseen half the medical crews operating out of over two hundred fire stations dotted across Manhattan. There was no chance she could outrank this superstud of emergency medicine. And yet again she'd given him the upper hand by admitting that he had not one, but two things she wanted.

She gritted her teeth. Something was going to have to give. Either she was going to have to find some way to work with this Mr. Goody-Rescue-Boots, or act on her years-old threat to pack up her surfboard and find a new shore.

As those thoughts rattled uncomfortably from her head down to her heart, Zach's demeanor shifted from defensive to composed, with the clear arrival of a light bulb moment. His stupid eyes were ridiculously expressive. A perfect window into his deep and incredibly detail-oriented thought-process.

This was not the lifeless, gimlet-like lizard

gaze of his predecessor. No, Zach's eyes were more like a kaleidoscope. Dark sapphire-blue when he was angry—which he had been when they'd first met—and shot through with shards of flint when he had made up his mind about something. They were bright, like the sea beyond the reef, when he reached a place of understanding. As he had now.

The well-defined lines of his facial features relaxed into a strangely comforting expression. One that spoke of having hit a thousand rocky shores but, fueled by willpower alone, having found a way to pull himself out of the fray.

Every. Single. Time.

For heaven's sake. Even his emotional scar tissue was better than hers.

"It's a big house for one person," she muttered, hoping the comment would serve as a concession that, yes, she got that it was his—but, no, she wasn't quite ready to buy him a housewarming present.

"I didn't buy it solely for myself," he said.

His tone was not exactly apologetic, but she could sense that he was sorry she was hurt. Which, of course, flicked off another plate from her armor. People who had compassion were impossible to be furious with.

She narrowed her eyes and tried to scan him for glimpses of insincerity, hoping he'd learned that pacifying technique in a management class.

Nope. It was organic. Real. He actually genuinely did look as though it bothered him that he'd upset her.

She absently traced some lines into the sand between them, realizing too late that she'd drawn a heart. She swiped it away with her foot before he could notice, then met his gaze. "Well, I hope you and your wife enjoy it."

His eyes darkened to near black, then cleared. "It's just me and my son," he said, his voice unnaturally bright. Or…no… It was affection. Protectiveness. The same way her brothers would say, *Oh. You've met Lulu, have you? She's my kid sister.* Two parts love to one part *If you do a single thing to hurt her…*

There was definitely a story there.

Something in her softened. She should probably cut the guy some slack. After all, he hadn't exactly been sent a memo warning him that he'd taken both her job *and* her house.

"Hey," he said, after a quick glance at his

watch. "I've got to get back to the house. My parents are looking after my boy and I said I'd be back by now. We haven't unpacked anything yet... I don't know if it would rub salt in the wound, or serve as what it's intended to be—a peace offering—but maybe you could show us somewhere good to eat? My shout. It might give us a chance to..." His lashes brushed his cheeks as he lowered his eyes to choose his words. He looked back up at her. "I think we need a do-over in the first-impressions department."

A rush of excitement and half a dozen options flew to mind and, rather surprisingly, she felt a warm, happy smile replace the tense scowl she'd been wearing. Wednesday was two-for-one burger night at the Moo Oink Quack Shack.

"Burgers suit?" she asked, quickly adding, "They cater to all types. There's tuna, turkey, beef, pork and taro if you're veggie."

She gave his lean yet muscular physique a quick scan, trying to determine if someone that solid could be made of mushrooms and spinach. Her eldest brother was a vegan and he could pull a car down the road if necessary, so anything was possible really.

"Sounds good. I know Harry, my boy, will definitely be on board for a turkey burger."

"A carnivore, is he?" Lulu grinned and patted her tummy. "A man after my own heart. I like a boy who knows what he wants from life."

Something shadowed Zach's features, then slipped away before she could define it. He pointed toward a bright red convertible Jeep parked under a stand of palms shading the staff parking lot. He had, she could see, parked in the chief's spot.

"Can I give you a ride?"

"I've got my own, thanks. Shall I lead the way, seeing as you're a newbie on the island?"

"That'd be a big help. I'm still working on getting my bearings here."

Zach folded into a courtly bow. When he rose and met her eyes, she saw what she hadn't seen before. A kind man. A worthy man. Someone who was starting over after having been brought to his knees by an unexpected blow. As blindsided by life's cruelty as she'd been when her parents had died.

She turned away before he could see her eyes fog with the tears she'd sworn she'd never spill, semi-audibly muttering something about getting her backpack and keys.

Urgh. Now she had compassion for him as well.

Zach Murphy made hating him very, very difficult.

Shouldering her pack, emotions back in check, she tried to wipe the muddied shoreline of her mind clean, just as the tide swept the beach clean twice a day. It was a meditation thing her navy SEAL brother Kili did. He said if the beach could start over twice a day so could he.

Sure, he'd been talking about making it through boot camp with a broken arm at the time… But Lulu was sure the theory could be applied to rotten first impressions.

She totally got the "fresh start" thing. She saw it a lot on the island. *Haoles* arriving from the mainland, hoping to change their lives for the better. To leave whatever it was that had turned their lives dark behind them.

Heaven knew she'd threatened her brothers with a move to the mainland where no one knew her—or them—enough times. It was always threat enough to get them to back down. For a bit, anyway. There was a part of her that lived in fear of the day when one of them would call her bluff. A day she hoped would never come. She loved it here. Loved her family. She missed her parents—her mom, in particular—in the same way she'd miss her own blood pumping through her veins, but…she had her memories.

She decided there and then not to make Zach's probation harder than it already would be. Then again, she thought as she pulled on her helmet and revved up her motorcycle, she wouldn't make it entirely easy…

"What are you? Hawaii's answer to Steve McQueen?"

Zach was laughing as he spoke, getting out of his Jeep, and he took Lulu's helmet from her after she'd tugged it off over her thick-as-molasses hair, but she could see a question in his eyes.

She couldn't help it. She bristled. Riding her bike was her happy time. Well… Surfing was her happy time. But when she wasn't in the water, riding her motorcycle was her happy time. Speed and a connection with all she held dear.

The thick, tropical air. The breeze off the ocean. The sharp scent of the coffee plantations they'd swept past (possibly at a mile or two above the speed limit). The warm, mouthwatering aroma of frying garlic about to be united with some gorgeous shrimp. The green jungle tang of unfettered growth as they'd passed Oahu's famed North Shore on the way to this quiet little slice of heaven she'd prayed she might one day call her own.

So, *Yeah, pal.* It was a big fat yes—because she'd driven to Turtle Hideaway at precisely the right speed. *Her* speed.

She already had five big brothers commenting on everything from the length of her hair to the shortness of her skirts. She didn't need to add a micromanaging boss to the mix. Even if he was as hot as blue blazes.

"That's Stephanie McQueen to you," she said with a grunt as she kicked the stand into place, trying to take as much of the bike's weight as she could as it fell into place.

Zach snorted good-naturedly, then sobered. "I thought fifty miles per hour was the maximum speed across the whole island?"

"You want to be a policeman now, as well? Solve crimes? The Five-O are always recruiting."

She winced at her tone. The comment had come out more snarky than jokey. "Okay. You got me." She held her hands wide, as if about to ask a universal question not even the wisest of souls could answer. "Who doesn't want to show off for the new boss?"

Zach's expression shifted to something inscrutably neutral, as if he were privately assessing her but saving his feedback for her staff assessment—which, annoyingly, he'd be giving her in a few weeks' time.

She might as well have told him she wanted to lick his sweaty chest then feed him grapes before they made mad, ferocious love under a moonlit sky.

Oh, man. Did she?

Kind of.

Maybe not the sweaty chest thing…but all the rest of it…

She rolled her eyes behind her lids, wondering if she should dig a hole now or wait for the earth to open up and swallow her whole.

If any of the Hawaiian gods were real, or helpful, or both, it would crack open any moment now.

She reminded herself of one of her grandmother's countless island proverbs. *Energy flows where attention goes.* If she kept drawing every-

thing Zach said to a dark or sexy space, the way
they related to one another would inevitably be
combative. Or sexy. Or both. And that was no
way to work with someone. Not with the job they
did. Pure synchronicity was essential. They had
to trust one another with their lives, and as such
there wasn't any room for negativity or out-of-
control hormones.

*You can't stop the waves, but you can learn
how to surf.*

Her father's favorite saying.

Pffft.

She already knew how to surf.

She reached out to take her helmet back from
Zach, scraping round for a new line of thought.
His problems would be better to focus on than
hers. What was it that had chased a man so in-
herently in control of things so very far away
from home?

"Daddy!"

A young boy—six years old, maybe seven?—
came running down the packed red earth path
that led to her—to *Zach's* new house. The boy's
gait was a bit off. He was up on tiptoe and his
arms windmilled as if he was constantly on the
verge of tripping over his own feet. She did a

lightning-fast scan of the boy as both she and Zach quickened their pace to meet him. His movements were definitely clumsy, and his hands weren't moving in sync with the rest of him.

"You're home!" the boy cried, virtually crashing into his father's solid wall of a chest for a big old bear hug. Just the type her brothers gave her when they knew she'd had a tough day.

Something about the way Zach hugged his son tight, bent down to kiss his wavy head of identical chestnut hair, pulled back to examine his face, then pulled him close again, brought a lump to Lulu's throat. There was real, genuine love there.

Sexy, smart *and* a good dad.

"Look!" Harry grinned up at his father and pointed at his mouth. His two front teeth were missing.

"Hey! I guess that means we're due a visit from the Tooth Fairy tonight." Zach's smile faltered. "Unless...you didn't have a fall, did you, big guy?"

Harry shook his head, his smile still very much from ear to ear. "No. They came out when I was eating watermelon. Grandma's got them in a jar."

"Ah, well, then. I'll be sure to give the Tooth Fairy a call once you've gone to bed tonight."

Zach held his hand up for a high five, which his son returned, but instead of just slapping the hand he held on to his father and started to do a little dance, jigging back and forth to the beat of a drummer neither Zach nor Lulu could hear.

Lulu couldn't help it. She giggled. This was one happy kid.

When Zach turned back to Lulu she saw that fatherly love had displaced everything else that had passed between them. His son was very clearly his here and now. His sun, his moon, his stars. His…yes…his Turtle Hideaway. And, though it was going to be tough to let that particular dream go, she knew right in the very center of her heart that the house had gone to someone who would love it and care for it as much as she did.

"Lulu?" Zach smiled down at his son, then back at her. "I'd like you to meet my boy. This is Harry."

Lulu squatted down so that she was at eye level with him and extended her hand. "How do you do, Harry?"

"I'm good, thank you." He grinned a huge happy,

gap-toothed grin. "Especially now that Daddy's back." He gave Lulu a bit of a jerky handshake then beamed up at his father.

Cerebral palsy. That was it. She would lay money on it. Not that it felt good coming to that conclusion. Life wouldn't be easy for Harry.

Once a month she worked with a charity that brought all sorts of disabled children out onto the waves, either on surfboards or canoes—or, in the case of some children with extremely severe disabilities, an extrahuge inner tube. She loved experiencing the rush of surfing along with a child who would never be able to experience it on their own.

Her heart cracked open another notch for Zach Murphy.

No wonder he was a rule-book guy.

"Come!" Harry grabbed Lulu by the hand and began to pull her down the path toward the house. "I want to show you my room!"

CHAPTER FOUR

ZACH ERASED THE concerns he'd had about Lulu not treating his son like she might any other little boy. A lot of people were knocked off their stride when they realized Harry had cerebral palsy. His wife, for example.

He shoved the thought back where it belonged. In the past. They'd made their peace. Their decisions. Their separate moves toward a happier future. Even so…he couldn't bear it when people didn't see the same things he saw when he looked at his little boy. A loving, bright kid, kiboshed by a critical absence of oxygen during the birthing process. Sure, he could've sued. But a wad of cash wasn't going to change his boy's life. Good parenting was. Shame his wife hadn't seen things the same way…

Zach followed Lulu and Harry along the path lined with well-established banana trees and rounded a small stand of palms to see the house. His smile broadened when he saw Harry enthusiastically pulling Lulu up the handful of steps onto the wraparound wooden porch that had been pretty much all he'd needed to see of the house before asking the Realtor to take down the for-sale sign.

Their view back in Manhattan had been of a brick wall. Now it was the Pacific Ocean. The fact this place hadn't been sold the second it went on the market was a miracle. So it was a bit of a fixer-upper? He wasn't afraid of a hammer and a nail. What he couldn't do, there were likely tradesmen around to help with.

Harry stumbled on the steps as he clambered to get to the top, which wasn't unusual. Zach's instinct was always to lurch forward and help, but he'd been trying to let his son learn from his own mistakes. One of the toughest lessons for a parent to grasp,

Harry stumbled again, slapping his hand down on the step and only just avoiding a few splinters in his knee. Instead of going into a hypercautionary mode, as many people did, Lulu laughed along with his son and, as if she were merely starting a new game, looped her arm through his for a spontaneous three-legged race to his bedroom—which, Zach realized, was her way of keeping Harry upright while providing him with a bit of dignity.

There was a clamor of voices in the living room as they entered. His parents. Rather than leap in and micromanage, as he might very well be accused of doing, he thought he'd try to give Lulu the space and respect to be the adult woman she was. His way of addressing the getting-to-know-you do-over.

He heard introductions. *Alohas*. His mother explaining that her real name was Francesca, but she preferred Frankie, and that Lulu was welcome to call her husband, Martin, Marty— everyone did. All of this was followed up by Lulu offering an explanation that her name was Polynesian for Pearl, but she found that far too girlie, and then, after Harry said something that made them all laugh, explaining the game they were playing. By the sounds of the thumping, the three-legged race was back on again.

Zach smiled.

Ten points to Lulu for dodging his mother's twenty questions. Another ten points for not calling out the special-needs kid for being a klutz. He'd always tried to keep his son's focus on what he *could* do, rather than what he couldn't.

It looked as though Lulu was cut from the same cloth.

He knew it shouldn't be a huge surprise, seeing as anyone was capable of being kind. It was just… He guessed the last few years and his disaster of a marriage had been a life lesson in learning that love didn't always come from the most obvious candidates.

Not that he had the whole perfect-parenting thing down to a tee—possibly, never would. He used to caution people. Warn them. Mention what to look for when interacting with Harry, what to try to ignore. He used to do it to his wife.

It had taken his marriage falling apart and a telling off from his son after a particularly overprotective school sports day for him to realize that all his cushioning made people treat Harry differently—whereas if they'd met his son without all the preamble, they would have been every bit as disarmed by the sheer amount of joy his gorgeous, sunny-dispositioned boy possessed.

He parked himself on the porch, eyes trained on the sun as it began its descent. In New York, the summer sun hung in the sky deep into the evening hours. Here it looked like it was lights-out around six thirty—give or take half an hour—no matter what time of year it was.

Equatorial life was going to take some getting used to. And he wasn't just talking about the sun.

His mother appeared and sat herself down next to him with a light pat on the knee.

"She seems nice… Lulu. Pretty, too."

He nodded but avoided eye contact. Ever since the divorce had become final a year back she'd been intent on getting him back into the dating game. No amount of *I'm not going there again, Mother* had put her off.

She was a feisty second-generation Italian woman who'd married a feisty second-generation Irishman. The pair of them regularly set off fireworks by rubbing together in both the right and the wrong ways. But most of all their relationship was big on love. They might never agree on the perfect wattage for a reading lamp light bulb, but they'd never let Zach down.

However, he could do without their help in the matchmaking department. He'd learned the hard way that a physical attraction to someone did not a long-lasting relationship make. So, no matter how…erm…*pronounced* a reaction his body had to Lulu, he was going to have to ignore it.

"How'd your first appearance at work go?" his mother asked, in a tone suggesting that she'd seen his thoughts running through his eyes like a ticker tape.

He gave a self-effacing grunt. "Not great."

His mother looked back over her shoulder to where they could hear Lulu making dinosaur noises with Harry. No prizes for guessing that Harry was showing her his new Lego collection. His ex had bought him a fire-breathing dinosaur kit as prep for life on Hawaii, only to discover that only the dinosaur *film* had been set here... There had never been actual dinosaurs.

"Facts schmachts," she'd said.

And therein lay one of their many differences. Zach liked his feet solidly grounded in reality, while Christina was a dreamer through and through. He'd thought it would work. Being a ying-yang couple. His parents couldn't be more different from each other, but they were always able to see things from the other's perspective, claiming their differences had made them stronger as a couple.

But that hadn't been the case with Christina. Their differences had been like tectonic plates destined to crack apart—the gap growing ever wider as the stresses and strains of life took their toll. Eventually, he'd had to face facts. They had a disabled son who would need help for the rest of his life and Christina didn't want to do it.

His mother tapped him on the knee and pointed out toward the bay, where a turtle was crawling up onto the beach. "There's Christopher."

"Christopher? How do you know? Are they tagged, or something?"

"No," she laughed. "It's what Harry's been calling all the turtles making an appearance."

A sting of guilt lanced his conscience. Back in New York, Harry's best friend was Christopher. His mother was a caregiver and she always took Harry in after school, or whenever Zach couldn't change his shifts to match his son's schedule.

It was one of the reasons he'd taken this nine-to-five job. Reliability. Sure, there would be the odd out-of-hours call, but the main point was, as he was the only one Harry had to rely on now, he wouldn't be risking his life at work the way he'd used to.

He made a mental note to take some pictures and send them back home. He stopped. Corrected himself. Back to New York. Their life was here now. With a bit of organization Harry and Christopher could have regular video calls. With a bit of ingenuity they could even have one from the beach, so they could show the real Christopher his new namesakes.

"I'm guessing you're going for the minimalist look?" Lulu appeared, laughing as she plonked herself down on the step next to Zach's mom, her elbows on her knees, leaning forward to catch his eye. "Or will you be building all of your furniture out of Lego?"

Zach gave her the thumbs up. "Got it in one."

She laughed. Their eyes cinched a bit tighter than they probably should have for a man and woman who'd hit it off so badly.

Zach broke the eye contact first and, because he was himself, explained, "I thought we'd go local on our purchases instead of shipping things in. We sold all of our furniture out East and..." He trailed off before he told the real truth.

He'd sold everything because he didn't want any reminders of his married life—apart, of course, from his son. Harry had been allowed to pack his favorite toys and books of course, but the bed Zach and Christina had once slept in...? *Uh-uh.* The kitchen table he'd knelt alongside to ask her to be his wife...? *Sold.* The gray sofa, side chairs and throw pillows she'd insisted upon buying, because gray was the new black? *No, thank you.* Blue skies, azure oceans and lush green mountains were his new color scheme and he liked it that way. He only prayed his boy did, too.

"Cool." Lulu genuinely sounded impressed. "If you want me to point you in the direction of some awesome local craftsmen, I'm more than happy to help."

"Well, now, that's a lovely offer—isn't it, Zachary?" Zach's mom said, her voice heavy with meaning. The kind that meant she'd happily offer to babysit if they wanted a joint shopping trip to involve some "adult time."

"Thanks." Zach pressed himself up to stand. "That'd be great. But right now..." He patted his belly. "I'm getting hungry, and Lulu here has been bragging on a local burger shack."

"Sure have." Lulu bounced up. "Are you and Mr. Murphy coming as well?"

"Frankie and Marty, dear," Zach's mom insisted, before throwing Zach an *I think this one's worth a few dates* look.

He only just managed to contain his eye roll

as he called his son to come on out to the porch. And his dad. They might as well all go.

Half an hour later they were all glowing in the remains of the day's sunlight, their newly arrived meal covering the bulk of a huge round picnic table parked at the high end of the beach, but chained to a nearby coconut palm "just in case."

"So?" Lulu asked after a few minutes of contented munching. "What do you think?"

"Amazing," Zach said through a mouthful of barbecued pork and pineapple burger. "Never had anything like it."

Lulu beamed proudly—as if she had been the one to slow roast it in the barbecue and griddle the pineapple herself. Local pride, he guessed. The same way a native New Yorker would swear on his life that he knew the best local pizzeria or, in his dad's case, the best Irish pub.

"I can't believe we've lived here all these years and never eaten here," Zach's father said, wiping a bit of mayonnaise off his cheek. "This hamburger is out of this world!"

Frankie agreed about her own burger and then, her eyes darting between Lulu and Zach, added, "It's fantastic to see Marty eat so much. When we eat out, we normally go to the officers' club."

She gave her husband a tender look, then said, "I haven't seen him devour anything they serve like this."

Lulu's brow furrowed. "The Naval Officers' Club?"

"Oh, no. Retired Fire and Rescue Officers'."

Zach's father jumped in. "What she's trying to say is we go to the same place too often. Don't explore enough." He coughed and then, turning away from the table, coughed some more.

Lulu didn't miss the creases of concern on Frankie and Zach's faces as Marty recovered, then turned back, his thin face wearing a *Nothing to see here* expression.

"Sorry 'bout that." He pointed at his throat. "A bit of a tickle. Anyhow, you were saying about exploring more...?"

Frankie gave her husband a pat on the arm. "We've lived on the island long enough to let go of our safety net. Perhaps Lulu will show us some more places like this now that we're all here."

Zach's eyebrows shot up to his hairline. Interesting... This would normally be the point where his mother hammered a poor, innocent woman with a thousand questions. Who were her parents? Where had she grown up? What were her hopes, her dreams? Was there anything they should know about her past? Her future?

Not this time. His mother was clearly taking a different tack. Deference. Trying to prove *they* were the ones worth considering. It was something he'd thought he might see when hell froze over, but certainly not before.

It had never occurred to him that their confidence might've been knocked by the move out here for his father's health.

Then again, it had also never occurred to him that some of his friends would stop returning his calls when his ex had filed for divorce.

Had his dad's fire station buddies done the same? Kept their distance once his dad's health prognosis had forced him into early retirement? It would've been a heck of a kick in the teeth after all the years of service and friendship his father had given.

He considered another possibility: that his parents had made the move in the way a wounded animal took itself far away from the pack to try its best to recover.

Neither option sat well.

He took a fry and swept it through some ketchup,

dropping it at the memory of how shocked he'd been when his parents had met them at the airport. His dad had lost a lot of weight in the few months since he'd seen them last, and that cough of his was gaining traction. He felt ashamed that he'd been so involved in his own life that he hadn't noticed just how much his father's health had degenerated.

Now that he'd found a job, made the move, bought a house and was in a place where he could start settling Harry in, he finally had the brain space to see the bigger picture. He wasn't the only one who needed help. His parents needed him here every bit as much as he needed them. They were all hurting. All trying to heal. And any ray of sunshine that came their way was worth its weight in gold.

His gaze instantly shifted to Lulu.

Even if it came in a five-foot-two-inch package of fire and electricity?

Before the thought could gain purchase, Harry lifted up his burger and oinked like a pig, mooed like a cow, then launched into his best chicken impression as they all began to laugh.

"I'll take that as a thumbs-up." Lulu laughed,

giving him that hand signal Zach had seen several times now.

"What *is* that?" he asked.

"What? This?" Lulu curled her hand into a loose fist except for her thumb and pinky finger and waved it back and forth. "It's the *shaka* sign."

"What does it mean?"

"Hang loose. *Aloha*. That's cool."

"All at once?"

"It symbolizes a shared respect."

She gave a light shrug before Zach could attach too much meaning to the comment.

"It's basically whatever you want it to mean. So long as its friendly," she added, with a small but perceptible upward tilt of her chin.

Lulu's eyes met his head-on. They were flame colored. It was easy enough to see that it was the sun making her eyes appear as if they had a life of their own, but Zach knew the fire that burned in them flared bright and hot with a note of warning. The *shaka* sign was the first thing she'd done when she'd met him, and what had he done in return? He'd barked an instruction. Then he'd made it worse. Belittled her in front of her crew and the people they'd just rescued.

It had been a careless thing for a new chief to do and, more to the point, unkind and lacking in respect. The fact she'd agreed to come over to the house he'd unwittingly bought from under her *and* had been kind to his son and parents meant one thing and one thing only.

He owed her an apology.

He lifted up his hand and tucked his fingers into the sign. "Is this right?" He shook his hand back and forth, his eyes not leaving hers.

"Bit stiff," she said, trying and failing to keep a straight face. "You'll get there."

"You think so?"

She shrugged, then said in a sonorous voice, "Watch, and you will learn how to do it."

Zach frowned. "That's exactly what I did."

Lulu rocked back on her bench seat and laughed. "No, bruh. That's something my grandmother says. She's got, like, a thousand 'true Hawaiian' sayings. Most of them are probably made up... but sometimes there's a lot of sense in them."

"Oh, yeah? Like..." He opened his hands for her to continue then took another bite of his burger.

Lulu eyed him for a minute, as if deciding exactly which of her grandmother's sayings best suited the man and the moment.

"'You are a chief *because* of your people.'"

The words hit him where they'd been aimed. Right in the solar plexus.

"Good advice," his dad said, when Zach failed to reply. He gave the picnic table a thump with one hand and lifted his burger with the other and then, before he took a bite, stopped himself and nodded at Lulu and at Zach. "You're lucky to have this one on your team, son. You two make a good match."

They were a match, all right. Whether or not they were a good one only time would tell.

And with that the sun dropped behind the horizon, preparing itself to reappear on the other side of the island tomorrow morning, when they would begin again. And this time Zach knew he'd be pouring his all into trying to get it right.

CHAPTER FIVE

WITH THE ALERT radio turned up to high volume, Lulu went outside to see if the inevitable storm clouds had gathered to break the day's intense humidity. Though she'd grown up with it, even she was feeling the closeness of this final day in August.

Today she was on dispatch duty, while the rest of the team performed what Zach referred to as "team building." It was the type of team building she was pretty sure in any other parlance was called cleaning.

Yesterday they'd team built the helicopter until it glinted in the sun. Today's focus was nautical. The speedboat and the RIB needed a scrubdown. The equipment needed checking over. Ropes and harnesses needed to be examined and repaired if necessary. It was the same kind of stuff she imagined they did at the firehouses and EMT headquarters back in New York—not because it was nice when things were shiny and clean, but because lives depended on it.

Her ear still tuned in to the radio, she wandered under a small clutch of palms, staying tucked mostly out of sight from the rest of the crew, who were farther down the stretch of grass just above the beach where they kept the boats. Laughing, talking, throwing jokes and good-natured insults back and forth, they were clearly having a good time.

It was a nice change from when Clive had run the crew. He'd been... Well, she was sure he'd been nice enough back in the day, but she was also pretty sure that when he'd been assigned crew chief of their specialist search and rescue team he'd very clearly mistaken the modern world for the 1950s.

Being treated like little more than a coatrack when her specialty was emergency rescue and medicine had been quite a blow. And she had to admit Casey hadn't fared much better. But Casey was a whole lot better at doing the water-off-a-duck's-back thing. She might look like a beauty queen, but she was shot through with a core of steel.

Lulu gave her shoulders a shake, willing herself to literally and figuratively shake it off. Clive was gone now. Fishing, probably. Or napping. And, after a few heaven-sent weeks of proving to the guys that she had what it took to run the crew, she was "back in her place."

She silently chided herself for instantly going to the glass-half-empty scenario.

She stared down at her hands, forcing a bit more honesty to surface.

Zach wasn't as bad as she'd initially thought. Quite the opposite, in fact.

Divorced, his mother had whispered when she'd been over at their house the other day. *Knocked him sideways*, she'd managed, before Zach had come in to find them, no doubt trying to stem the passing of sensitive information.

It had added another layer to what little she knew about him. A level of complexity she hadn't gleaned from his opening *Me Boss, You Employee* maneuver.

No, Zach Murphy was definitely more than what you saw at first glance.

He liked things shipshape, but he didn't delegate. He joined in. Expected as much from himself as he did from the others. And, despite the whole *You're grounded* thing, he didn't seem at all focused on keeping her away from the big-boy jobs like Clive had. He already had them on a roster that was as egalitarian as it came. Alphabetical.

It could be tactical. In their small crew it didn't take long to see who came after Lulu Kahale.

That's right. Mr. Zachary Murphy.

Another huge burst of laughter came from the guys. Lulu looked across, felt her breath hitching at the base of her throat as her eyes landed on her new boss just as he was pulling his top off.

Oh, my.

It looked like a torso-of-the-week photo shoot.

Her tooth snagged on her lower lip as Zach grabbed the hose, tipped back his head and ran the cool water over himself. Her eyes were jealously glued to the stream of splashing liquid as it poured down his toned body.

Yum.

The politically correct part of her brain that was in a fury anytime she was treated differently because she was a woman knew she shouldn't be treating Zach's team-building exercise as a chance to appreciate his physical attributes, but... *Mmm...* Her hormones were overriding all normal brain functions.

It had been quite a while since she'd had a date, let alone a boyfriend, and Zach Murphy was exceedingly good-looking. Strong, but not bodybuilder bulky. His hair had gone from lightly wavy to extrawavy, thanks to the humidity. It was longer than a buzz cut, but not so long you'd mistake him for a transient surfer dude.

Which made her wonder... Did he surf? Was that a thing out East? His fluidity of movement suggested he'd be strong in the water if they needed an extra rescue swimmer. He'd not gone on any of their rescues yet, claiming he wanted to get a grip on the paperwork, discover the lay of the land before he went out with them. Instead, he'd put Lulu in charge.

Publicly, she'd said the decision was an obvious nod to the fact she'd been helming the team since his predecessor had officially retired to his hammock. Privately, she felt ridiculously proud that he had even an ounce of trust in her after their first very false start.

He could have easily made an example of her. Suspended her back on Day Zero. He'd been right. She hadn't been in regulation gear. She'd left the office open. The medicine cabinet and gear were obviously locked up...but sometimes thieves didn't care about things like that. And, of course, there were the piles of undone paperwork that he was wordlessly plowing through, knowing damn straight she should've done it.

So, yeah... Right now, she really wanted to put her best foot forward.

It was a rare chance to be judged for her merits alone, rather than being mollycoddled and then ignored because of the "talking-to" her brothers had given Clive.

Something told her that even if her brothers did get to Zach, he'd hear them out, because he was fair that way, but he wouldn't be swayed by them.

One of the guys cracked a joke, winning a rare but heartfelt guffaw from Zach. He wasn't the most carefree of men...but his smiles could knock your socks off. If you were into that sort of thing.

In fact... Lulu scraped her teeth across her lip. If it weren't for the fact his two front teeth were crooked, he'd almost be too good-looking. Which was one of the many things on her no-go list when it came to considering potential dates. That tiny "flaw," such as it was, made him mortal. Which meant he was accessible to other mere mortals...like herself.

Hmm... Perhaps she should recommend one of the island's better orthodontists.

"Here's your shaved ice, girlfriend." Casey appeared by her side and handed her a palm leaf bowl filled with her favorite flavor—coconut and mango. She'd been out filling up the crew jeep's gas tank and obviously felt blasted by the weather as well. "What are we looking at?"

Lulu feigned an indifference she definitely didn't feel. "Just watching the boys doing some of the clean-up work for a change."

Casey snorted appreciatively. She leaned on the canoe Lulu had propped herself against, watched for a few moments, then shouted out, "Keep up the good work, boys!"

They laughed, waved and offered invitations to join in.

"Lunch break," Lulu parried, raising her shaved ice.

A volley of good-natured insults flew their way, melting in the heat before they landed. Lulu and Casey continued watching the guys at work the way they might watch a documentary on dolphins. Completely rapt.

"He's not as bad as we thought he was going

to be, is he?" Casey nudged Lulu's foot with her flip-flop.

"Who?" Lulu asked, knowing exactly who Casey was talking about.

Casey tipped her head down and looked at her over her sunglasses. "Don't be stupid."

"I'm not!" Lulu protested hotly. Too hotly, judging from Casey's cackled response.

"You haven't looked at anyone like that in the history of me knowing you," she teased.

"That's not true! There was—" Lulu sought her memory for just one of her short-term boyfriends who had made goosebumps ripple up her arms in the middle of a summer's day and came up blank. Rather than admitting as much she offered Zach a backhanded compliment. "He definitely knows how to keep the bosses back on the mainland happy. Does the paperwork as if his life depended on it."

Casey shrugged. "Maybe it does."

Lulu kicked off her flip-flops and dug her toes into the sand. Casey might've nailed it.

As much as she'd wanted to find flaws in him after that first awful impression…she was struggling. When he'd invited her to his house—*her* house—she'd been prepared to play the happy islander right up until they were settled at the burger shack and then she was going to read him the riot act. Let him know how things really worked in Hawaii.

And then she'd met Harry. Funny, kind, a brilliant dinosaur impersonator and quite clearly the keeper of the solitary key to Zach Murphy's heart.

His parents were great, too. They probably had spare keys… Warm-hearted. Friendly. Eager to learn more about Hawaii. His dad had a worrying cough, but she hadn't felt it was appropriate to ask about it.

There'd been no mention of Harry's mother, and despite some rather epic earwigging over the past week she'd been unable to figure out why Zach's marriage had failed. One thing she was sure about: he wasn't much of a talker. Definitely an actions-speak-louder-than-words kind of guy. And, from what he'd done over the past week, also respectful, conscientious, hardworking. He was—as she'd admitted to herself late last night, when she might have been accidentally-on-purpose thinking about him—about a million times better than her initial impression.

He turned, saw her watching him, and winked.

A million and one times?

She caught herself smiling in response. He returned the smile. A dimple appeared on his left cheek. It was cute. It ranked up there with that seemingly untamable cowlick at the back of his head. And, of course, those bright blue eyes of his.

Then she felt something cold land on her collarbone.

Ah. Her shaved ice.

He hadn't been winking at her—he'd been signaling to her that she was about to become a victim of her own ogling. Which, of course, hadn't been *ogling*. It had been...critical observation.

She frowned and turned away, trying to shake off the feelings as she swiped at the shaved ice. This wasn't like her. Not even close. She wasn't a flirter. And definitely not someone who dated. Well... She *dated*, but things never really moved beyond that. Either her brothers freaked the guys out by casually mentioning how much they could bench-press, or she nipped it in the bud before anything too close to feelings got involved.

It didn't take a psychiatrist to tell her that her idea of true love had been well and truly screwed up the day her father had grabbed his surfboard and paddled out to sea in the middle of storm to find their mother. His actions had declared one thing and one thing only: you should only marry someone you would risk your life for.

Not so great if you were their little kid, standing on the beach, holding your big brother's hand, wondering when Mommy and Daddy were going to come back, but hey… Whoever had named the Pacific Ocean for its peaceful nature had been having one hell of a laugh.

When she turned around Zach's back was to her and his fingers were hitched on his lean hips as one of the guys started pointing out something about the motor.

It was one of her favorite Zach poses—Zach with his fingers hitched on his hips. There was also the thinking pose, of which there were variations. Thinking with a head scrub. Thinking with a chin rub. Thinking while looking out to the ocean. Then there was Zach at her—*his*—desk. With a pencil tucked behind his ear. With a pen tracing along that deliciously full mouth of his. With his mouth parted as if he were just on the brink of—

Absolutely nothing.

She took a big bite of shaved ice, instantly giving herself a full-on case of brain freeze. Just as well. She would not and could not let herself crush on the new chief from the mainland. Swooning over him was too close to actual feelings, and feelings always got you in trouble. Just when she properly fell for him he would leave. Or she would get fired for inappropriate behavior. Or worse. As if there was anything "worse" than being fired.

A broken heart?

Pffft. She'd consigned her heart to the walk-in freezer of lost opportunities long, long ago.

As she sucked a few crystals of flavored ice off her knuckle their eyes met again. Something flared hot and bright between them, blurring out the rest of the world.

A flash image of a pair of his 'n' hers surfboards propped against the outdoor shower wall at Turtle Hideaway blinded her as the look intensified.

She rubbed her eyes to make it go away.

Insane fantasies like living with Zach were just that…fantasies. Mainlanders moved here convinced they wanted island life. But in the end all they actually needed was a monthlong vacation.

A surge of something that felt an awful lot like disappointment swept through her.

"Did you just sigh?" Casey asked.

"Ha!" She scoffed. "No."

Had she?

"OMG!" Casey cackled. "You totally did."

Lulu glared at her.

"You have the hots for him, don't you?" Casey asked, laughing as Lulu's cheeks pinked up.

"I totally do not."

Casey began laughing even harder. "You so completely do!" But as quickly as her laugh had begun, she went dead sober. "Don't you date him. You know you've got a trail of broken hearts in your wake and he's a good boss. We need to keep him here—and not just because he's a tasty bit of eye candy."

Lulu made a gagging noise. "As you very well know, I have rules. I don't date mainlanders. I don't date *haoles*. Nor do I date colleagues. Especially not a *haole* mainlander boss who buys my dream house. Just because he's sexy as a cake topper, it doesn't mean I'm going to rip his pants off, tear his heart out of his chest and dine on it for supper."

"Good to know," came a voice from behind her.

A very male and impossible to interpret voice that could only belong to Zach Murphy.

Awesome.

She turned around, doing her best to make her expression appear casually indifferent rather than completely mortified.

"I have high standards," she answered, as loftily as she could. That and she was scared to death of ever finding out what it was actually like to love someone.

"Hmm…" He hooked his fingers onto his hips. "Just as a matter of curiosity, is it a general Hawaiian thing not to date newcomers from the mainland, or something that's specific to you?"

His eyes didn't leave hers even though Casey was standing right there.

"Depends who's asking," she shot back.

"Asking what?" Stewart asked, joining them under the shady palms.

"Lulu here is giving Zach the rundown on her list of rules in order for her to date someone," Casey said.

"Oh, is she, now?" Stewart leaned against a palm, placing one food against it as a ballast. "I don't think I've ever known our Lulu not to stomp all over some poor unsuspecting suitor's heart." He crossed his arms over his chest and grinned. "This I would very much like to hear."

"Hear what?" another one of the other guys from the crew asked.

"Lulu's dating rules," Stewart said, pulling open a cool box and tossing cold bottles of water to everyone.

Lulu felt streaks of red working their way up from her chest to her collarbones then her neck, virtually strangling her as they burned their way across her cheeks. How completely mortifying.

"Are they your rules or your brothers' rules?" asked Kenji, aka Ken the Fin.

"I make up my own rules," Lulu retorted, unwillingly drawn into a conversational vortex she very much did not want to be in.

Everyone but Zach laughed.

Stewart took a swig of water and nodded at Zach. "Have you met the Kahales?"

He shook his head.

They all laughed again, shaking their heads and murmuring variants on, "Oh, this I gotta see!" And, "I hope someone's got a camera when that happens!" Or, "When's the Oahu tug-of-war again?"

"Will you guys shut up?" Lulu snapped. And then, to Zach, "Not you."

They laughed even harder.

Lulu saw red. "Oh, my God, you guys! Can it! If he was the last person on earth I wouldn't go out with Zach Murphy—all right?"

Too late, Lulu realized she'd screamed her little announcement aloud, and not in her head like a smart person would've done.

The team barely bothered hiding their snorts and guffaws behind their fists. Casey pretended to look slightly apologetic, but didn't really. And Zach looked bemused rather than hurt, which was even more irritating than the guys laughing.

Didn't he think she was worth dating? She knew she wasn't exactly bachelorette of the year, but it wasn't like she was grotesque. There'd been something between them just a few minutes ago. Enough to make him wink at her, anyway.

"Right. That's settled, then," Casey said, with a hand-wiping gesture that indicated the matter was closed to discussion. "We can all get back to work now, secure in the knowledge that Lulu and Zach will never, ever go on a date."

And just like that it was the only thing Lulu wanted to do.

* * *

Zach kept his gaze neutral, but he was wishing like hell he'd opted for the phone call version of this meeting with his boss instead of a video conference.

"You *what*, now?" he asked, instead of swearing.

"We'd like you and Lulu Kahale to represent the company at the Intra-Island Search and Rescue Games. Work out any problem points the two of you might have in advance."

"In advance of what?" he asked, instead of tearing the actual hair out of his head.

"The nationals," his boss said, as if it were obvious. "Of course there are also the International Search and Rescue Games to aim for, but we thought we'd start local."

What the actual—

"Sorry. I'm not following. You want me to play games with Lulu?"

He grimaced. That had come out all kinds of wrong.

His boss gave an easy laugh. The kind of laugh a man who delegated on a regular basis gave when asking someone to move a pyramid from one side of the desert to the other by the end of the week.

"It's a thing between the Coast Guard and the police force rescue squads. We thought we'd enter you all this year, to get some more visibility for the squad. See if we can attract some more investors. Long story short—you two have to win. No pressure."

If he could've volunteered to move a pyramid instead he would've done it, but Zach forced himself to smile and nod as his boss explained that the games would be held on the Big Island, where he and Lulu would stay in a hotel. Together. The games would take place over a long weekend in two weeks' time and would require the pair of them to work together "like a newly serviced sports car."

Zach only just managed to bite back a comment about how sports cars had a reputation for breaking down. Instead he smiled and nodded. He had never considered himself a yes-man, but two more months to go on his probation meant he wasn't in a position to say no.

He could, however, offer alternative suggestions. "Wouldn't someone who's been on the team a bit longer be better?"

"Nah," his boss replied, without bothering to think about it. "We've already done some research on the optics and the two of you make a good fit."

An image of Lulu that only belonged in the privacy of his bedroom cracked Zach's brain in half.

He shifted in his chair, trying to stem the images, while his boss rattled off a few ideas, then said he'd put it all in an email and zap it over so he and Lulu could hold a "blue sky meeting" about it.

"What? You want us to come up with ideas?"

"No. We want you to train together. Day and night. Let the rest of the crew put you through your paces. In two weeks' time you two must be on the same page—the *Oahu Search and Rescue are the winners* page. We want you to make one hell of an impression, if you get my meaning."

Zach did. They had to win. If they didn't, that probation threat hung in the air like a guillotine.

Thanking his boss for the "opportunity to promote the team" and, of course, health and safety in Hawaii, he ended the call and dropped his forehead into his hands with a groan.

How on earth was he going to achieve synchronicity with Lulu when they currently re-pelled one another?

He'd thought he'd fixed things between them on that first day, but about a week in there had been that weird conversation with the crew talking about her brothers and dating. Zach's one big takeaway was that Lulu Kahale was not on the market for a boyfriend. And if she was she definitely wouldn't be knocking on his door.

A knock sounded and the office door opened.

Lulu.

He sucked in a sharp breath.

She bristled.

He tensed.

Their eyes met and sparks of flinty heat sprayed everywhere they shouldn't have.

"You got a minute, boss?"

She'd taken to calling him "boss"—which for some reason felt like an insult coming from her. A challenge.

"Absolutely. Come on in."

His desk was shoved up against the wall of the small office. The only other chair was right next to his. He held out his hand, gesturing for her to take a seat, just as she reached out to grab the back of it. Their fingers brushed. He felt as if he'd just stuck his hand in a candle flame. As tempting as it was dangerous.

She took the chair and pulled it a couple of feet away from him before she sat down, dropping her staff backpack between them.

Subtle.

Neither of them said anything for a minute, as if each of them was braced for round twenty-seven, or whatever it was, of the weird hate-tinged game of *I respect you but only as far as I can throw you* they'd been engaged in for the past few weeks.

"How'd the hiker from this morning get on at the hospital?" he finally asked.

Lulu tilted her chin up. She'd been the one to belay down from the helicopter to get the twentysomething hiker onto a stretcher. "Good. A bit shaken up. Fractured wrist and a few scrapes and cuts."

"Did you manage to figure out how he'd ended up on that outcrop?"

She shrugged casually, as if novice hikers were always falling off the sides of mountains and needing rescuing. "Bird-watching through binoculars. Wasn't looking where he was going." She sniggered. "He was more annoyed that he hadn't been able to figure out what type of bird it was than anything else. Oahu Elepaio."

"What's that?"

"The bird."

"Oh! You saw it?"

"Nah. Heard it."

He nodded, impressed. Athletic, competitive, beautiful—and able to identify birdsong. What other hidden talents lay beneath Lulu's implacable surface?

He silently made the question rhetorical. He didn't want to know.

They sat and stared at one another for a moment, the conversation drying up as it often did on the rare occasions they were alone.

"So!" He clapped his hands together too loudly, not quite ready to tell her about his call with the boss. "What can I help you with?"

"Nothing," she said, her eyes darting round the office that had once been hers.

He hadn't changed it much. Not at all, really— except for making it a bit tidier. Maybe that was what this was. A power play. A dethroned lioness prowling round the new leader of the pride.

The word struck a chord. She was a lot of things, but above them all she was a proud woman. This wasn't some false bravura or macho grandstanding. It was pride. And he liked that about her.

He liked a lot of things about her.

That long, thick braid that swung between her shoulder blades. That nook between her jaw and her neck. The way her tooth dug into her lip when she was biting back something she clearly wanted to say. But they were colleagues. *End of.*

After the ticking of the clock grew too loud to tolerate, he tried again. "So…did you come in here to point that out, or is this your way of saying you'll get the paperwork from this morning to me later?"

A wash of guilt and then delight rippled across her features. A look of triumph took purchase as she pulled her backpack off the floor and presented him with a clipboard thick with completed forms.

"Here you are."

He flicked through the papers. "Looks like it's all here."

"Should be. I went over it twice."

He looked up and met her eyes in time to catch a hint of vulnerability. A desire to please. And it felt personal.

This time he was the one to push his chair back.

"Is Harry around this weekend?" Lulu asked.

"Yes," Zach answered cautiously. "Why?"

"I wanted to take him out surfing."

Before Zach could explain the number of reasons why that was an insane idea, she continued.

"I thought since he likes the turtles so much he could see what it feels like—you know, to fly on water. Not that turtles fly."

She rolled her eyes at herself. Small streaks of red were beginning to color her cheeks, as if she were silently willing herself to stop talking. But she didn't.

"I work for this charity. Well...not work. My brother and I volunteer there sometimes. We take special-needs kids out when we know the surf is going to be mellow. We've got special supports for kids with big physical hurdles, but I think Harry'd be good going out with me...so long as we slather him in sunblock. That kid is pale!"

Zach stared at her, then said, "He's not great at swimming."

"He doesn't have to be. We've got wetsuits, float vests, buoyancy aids. Everything he'll need." Her eyes flicked to his, the liquid amber irises a deep burnished gold. "He'll be safe with me."

Zach didn't know why, but he believed her. Which was huge. He'd never felt Harry would be safe when his ex-wife took him out. Especially when their outings were "visitations." Which was insane, because she was his mother, but...

A twist of acid stung his throat. Harry's cerebral palsy had closed something off in her—something he'd thought all mothers felt for their children, no matter what. An unbreakable, protective love.

"You can come, too." Lulu said, her eyes leaving his when he said nothing. "I mean, you have to, really, because I'll be taking other kids out, too. But..." She held her hands out in a *The choice is yours* gesture.

The invitation hung between them, and just as he saw her begin to adjust her posture, ready to take it back, he said, "Sounds great. We'd love to."

Her face broke into a broad grin. "Really? Awesome. Because I've already signed him up and your parents think it's a great idea."

"My parents?"

"Yeah, I—" Her expression turned hesitant. "I dropped by their condo the other day and talked to them about it. Floated the idea."

"You went to my parents' condo and talked to them about taking my son surfing?"

Lulu nodded slowly, tensing her body as if waiting for him to blow up. "Yes. Was that a bad thing to do? I was bringing them the addresses for some food trucks I thought they'd like."

Zach gave his head a double-handed scrub, then laughed. Properly laughed. He'd thought she hated him. People who hated someone didn't drop by their parents' house with top tips for taco trucks and offers to take their disabled son surfing.

Maybe he'd been looking at it all wrong. Lulu was a strong, proud, hard-working woman. She'd wanted his job. She'd wanted his house. He'd unwittingly swanned in and taken both. So she was regrouping. Figuring out how to let go of her plans for the future and move on.

"What? Why is that funny?"

"No. Lulu. Please… Sorry, I just—" Zach held his hand out, gesturing for her to take her seat again, which she did. Reluctantly. "Your offer is an amazing one. Generous. Kind. Yes, please. I'm sure Harry would love it. And I—" A knot of emotion suddenly rose and jammed in his throat as he pictured the scene. The beach, the sea, his boy on a surfboard… "I'd love for Harry to have that experience."

There were a thousand other things he'd love to see Harry enjoy, but this would be a damn good start.

Lulu rose, her smile more cautious this time, but still a smile. "That's great. So… I'll pick you both up at six on Saturday."

"On the motorcycle?"

She snorted. "I think you'll find the Highway Code doesn't allow three people on the back of a motorcycle."

He tapped the side of his nose. "Good to know."

He enjoyed her smile. Not smug from being right, but satisfied to have proved she knew the rules as well as he did.

"I have a Jeep," she said.

He nodded. It suited her. As much as the bike did. "So, that's six a.m., then?"

She rolled her eyes good-naturedly. "We're not going night surfing, boss."

"Zach," he corrected. If he was going to trust her to take his son out into the ocean, he wanted to be on a first-name basis with her.

She scrunched her nose for a second and didn't repeat his name. Just nodded. She backed up to the door frame, as if turning her back on him would make her too vulnerable. And as she left, with that soft smile of hers and an over-the-shoulder wave, he suddenly saw the invitation for what it truly was. An olive branch.

She'd gone before he remembered the Intra-Island Search and Rescue Games.

He should run after her and explain it all, but the moment they'd just shared had felt like a fresh start. A chance for a genuine friendship.

Something deep in his gut told him friendship with Lulu was hard-earned and precious. And he didn't want to do a single thing to compromise it.

CHAPTER SIX

LULU'S HEART WAS hammering in her chest. She couldn't believe she was doing this. Bringing Zach and Harry to the Superstars Surf Club. Her *brother* was going to be there. She didn't want Makoa to see her with Zach. He knew her tells. Her blushes. Her hair flicks. The way she covered all of it up with an extra splash of *I don't care what anyone thinks of me.*

But what was even bigger was the fact that Zach had agreed to come. The tension between them might have relaxed a bit, but she knew he still thought of her as a wild card. Someone to keep an extra eye on.

And now Zach was going to trust her with his son?

He's not Zach, she silently corrected herself. *He's your boss.*

Calling him Zach felt like entering a completely different, touchy-feely universe. Ultra-personal. The kind of personal that would give oxygen to the feelings that had all but consumed her since Casey had forced her to scream about not wanting to date him.

It was like she'd been cursed. Zach Murphy was in her brain nearly every second of every minute of every single shift they worked together. And pretty much all of the other minutes of the day since he'd walked out onto that pier and she'd tumbled headlong into those blue eyes of his. It was as if they'd swallowed her whole then spat her back out. She was someone she didn't recognize. Stupidly hungry to impress, strangely coquettish and ruled by a tummy filled with overactive butterflies that didn't seem to know when enough was enough.

These were teenage-girl-crush feelings. And now she was inviting him on one of her favorite days of the month to one of her favorite places on earth, where her brother would see her blushing like an idiot every time Zach Murphy laid eyes on her.

She pulled into the drive, not resenting the familiarity of the approach to the house as much as she had that first time she'd yanked her motorcycle onto the private little lane that led to Turtle Hideaway.

Knowing Harry was down here, tucked behind the palms and loving the little beach cove almost as much as she did, was an unexpected salve. Knowing the same about Zach was… Well, he hadn't yet announced any plans to knock the house down and replace it with some sort of chrome and steel number, like a lot of other mainlanders did to the traditional beach houses. That was something.

To her surprise they were already outside and waiting for her—rolled-up towels under their arms, board shorts on, smiles on their faces. What she could see of them, anyway. Both Zach and Harry were wearing snorkels and masks.

She'd barely brought her open-topped Jeep to a halt before Harry was doing his high-speed tiptoe running toward her. Her instinct was to get him to put the brakes on before he slammed into the side of the Jeep, but she'd hung around enough special-needs kids to know cushioning all the blows was worse than a few cuts and bruises.

Zach jogged behind him, tugging off his mask. Their eyes connected with a glint of mutual understanding that unleashed a warm glow of satisfaction in her chest.

Mahalo, he mouthed. *Thank you.*

He might as well have said *I want you* from the response it elicited. Her entire body was having a hot, tingly, glitter party. She'd never felt her clothes touch her body the way they were touching her now. Her T-shirt was brushing against her breasts, her cut-off jeans were brushing the tops of her thighs. Even her flip-flops brushed against the bottoms of her feet as if she were receiving her very first erotic foot rub.

"Load up—we're late," she said, instead of *I think I love you*—which, of course, would have been insanity. She didn't love Zach Murphy. She was crushing on him. Hard. But that was a hundred percent superficial and could be quashed with some concentrated mind over matter. He was her boss. And just because her entire body felt more alive than it had in years, that did not equate with a deep lifelong love. Certainly not the kind her parents had experienced.

"The moment I saw her... I knew."

And they'd wed two weeks later.

Lulu and Zach had known each other for five weeks and could barely be in the same room together, let alone on the same island, so it was pretty clear the two of them had nothing on her parents' love. Nor was this cloud cuckoo land.

She revved the engine and reversed out of the drive, doing her damnedest to ignore the fact that Zach had sat in the back seat. Right smack-dab in the center of her rearview mirror.

Twenty minutes later they were down at the beach.

Harry and Zach climbed out of the Jeep and followed Lulu up a small bluff, from where they could see the crowd on the beach.

Zach stopped in his tracks. "Wow."

Lulu beamed. She always felt that weird kind of teary happy on Superstars Surf Club day, and today was no different.

"I didn't expect there to be so many people," Zach said, his voice a bit scratchier, a bit deeper than normal.

"It's pretty amazing, isn't it?"

Below them on the beach was a crowd of about sixty or seventy people, about a third of them children, the rest of them family members and, of course, volunteers in their bright orange T-shirts.

"And do all these kids—"

"They've all got obstacles to surmount," Lulu

finished for him. "All sorts. Blindness, Down syndrome, autism, epilepsy, paralysis... But once they're out in the water with our volunteers—"

"None of it matters?" Zach finished for her.

"Exactly."

"Mini!"

Lulu cringed as Harry virtually leaped into his father's arms at the sound of her brother's huge foghorn of a voice.

"Mini-Menehune!"

She lasered her best evil eyes directly at her brother's chest. *Don't call me a magical dwarf!* And then caught herself adding, *Especially in front of Zach!*

"Hey! Mini! No *shaka* for the Mak-man?"

"Who's that?" Zach asked. "Friend of yours?"

"Brother," she growled.

She'd been hoping for a bit more time before Makoa spotted her, but that was the thing about her brothers. Always there when she both did and didn't need them. Her father's last words to Makoa had been *Look after your sister* and all five of them had taken the instruction to heart.

She popped on her brightest smile, hoping like hell that Mak would, for once, play it cool. "Hey, bruh! How's it hanging?"

"Great."

Her brother jogged up to them. Every insanely solid, muscled inch of his six foot five frame. He looked like a warrior with tattoos just about everywhere except his face. And that was only because their mother had made each of her sons promise that they'd never look battle-ready when she'd worked so hard to teach them the power of peace.

Makoa threw her a look. One that said, *You're being nice. What gives?*

She shrugged and nodded at Zach, as a reminder that they weren't alone.

Makoa rolled his shoulders back and turned to Zach. *"Aloha."*

Lulu was so used to men squaring themselves off against her brothers—each as big as the other—that she was more than quietly impressed when Zach stayed as he was, one arm casually slung over his son's shoulders, stance relaxed.

"Aloha," he said.

Her brother gave him the chin-lift and a *shaka* sign, then looked down at Harry. "Who's this little surfer man?"

Zach looked to his son. "Want to introduce yourself?"

Harry was staring up at Makoa as if he was Poseidon himself. In complete awe. Lulu was tempted to tell him that Mak's favorite dress-up outfit had been an old hula skirt and a coconut bra their mother had given them to play with as kids, but thought it best to let the moment play itself out. Her brother might drive her crazy, but he was a sucker for little kids, having three of them himself.

Mak knelt down, one knee on the sand, one tattooed forearm on his bent knee. He held out his hand. "I am Makoa. My friends call me Mak. You can call me Mak."

Harry beamed up at his father, then back at Mak. "I'm Harry. My friends call me...um... Harry."

"I like it." Her brother gave the boy's dark hair a scrub, then narrowed his gaze, as if inspecting him properly. He leaned forward conspiratorially and said, "You know, there was a King Harald. A Viking. A strong warrior of the sea. I bet you're like him. Show me your muscles!"

Mak struck a pose and then Harry did.

They all laughed. Lulu's brothers might be the most overprotective bears on the island, but moments like this reminded her that their hearts were made of solid gold. They also reminded her of how much she missed their big family gatherings. They were just so…complicated.

Did she show up with a plus one who would be put through her brothers' proverbial "boyfriend mangle"? Or did she show up single and endure the endless parade of men her brothers thought she should date?

She threw a surreptitious glance at Zach, who was still standing tall, relaxed and completely unintimidated by her big brother. Something tingled inside her. The unfamiliar heated spray of possibility.

Mak made a big show of being impressed by Harry's tiny little boy muscles, then challenged him to grab on to his flexed arm and be lifted up in the air. He swung him back and forth, much to Harry's delight and his father's concern.

Lulu knew that Zach had erased the crease in his brow before his eyes met hers, but she saw something there that she hadn't seen before. A core-deep need to protect his son at all costs, which sometimes involved stepping back and letting mishaps happen and at other times meant throwing himself in front of a speeding bus. It was a role that took precedence over everything.

Which made her wonder… What on earth had happened between him and his wife? Who could fail to be attracted to a man who honored his role as a parent so strongly? How on earth could you not want to do everything in your power to keep a kid this great safe and happy?

Whatever it was, there was definitely something dark and twisty keeping a stranglehold on Zach's free-and-easy side. It was a part of him she'd caught microglimpses of but had yet to properly unravel.

"So!" Mak pushed himself up to stand, his dark eyes still on Harry. "You looking forward to surfing with a champion today?"

Zach looked to Lulu. "Are you a champion surfer?"

Mak laughed. "I meant me."

"What?" Lulu bristled. Really? Just because he had one more measly medal than she did, he was pulling rank? "*I'm* taking Harry out. You take your own kids out."

She felt Zach's eyes zap to her as both he and Mak absorbed the protectiveness in her voice.

She knew Mak would use it against her. Tease her pretty much until the world ended. But Zach…?

She didn't know.

She barely knew his little boy, but they'd hit it off and she'd genuinely been looking forward to his first, inevitable laugh of delight when the wave and the board connected. When he recognized the harmony that came from working with the ocean's strength rather than against it. Watching a child who had the cards stacked against him realizing he could be just like everyone else… There was no better feeling than that.

"Chill, little sister." Mak patted her head as if she were a sweet-natured but not very bright dog. "I meant champion of the games."

Lulu felt her forehead crinkle underneath her brother's hand, which was still absently patting her head. "What games?"

"The Intra-Island Search and Rescue Games," he said, in a way that also said, *Are there any other games worth talking about?* He gave her head a final scrub, then reached out to shake hands with Zach. "I presume you're the new boss-man? I'm Makoa Kahale."

"Good to meet you." Zach shook her brother's hand, then threw Lulu a quick look she couldn't read.

"What's going on? Those games are between

the Coast Guard and your Ocean Safety lot, right?"

"Yes…" Mak drew the word out, then continued as if she were a simpleton. "And this year your little-bitty operation is in on the games."

"What?" Lulu looked at Zach and instantly saw that this was something he had known about and had actively chosen not to tell her. "Who's on the team?" she demanded.

"You are," Zach said, his blue eyes cinching with hers.

He looked nervous. Wary, even. As if he was waiting for a reproach for not having told her the instant he'd known. She didn't care. This was the best news since…since news had been invented.

"Are you kidding me? I'm on the team?"

She whooped and threw her arms around Zach, pressing her face against his chest before her brain caught up with her body and she pulled away.

He smelled good. Ocean, little boy…and maybe pineapple? He *felt* good, too. Strong, but lean. Not with that big monster-truck-style chest her brothers all had. And she wasn't positive, because her own heart had been hammering so hard, but she was pretty sure she'd felt his heart pounding through his T-shirt.

Panic? Or the same fizzy frisson she'd felt?

Whatever...

She started happy-dancing in front of her brother. "I'm gonna kick your booty!" She wiggled and shifted her dance toward Zach. "Who's going to be my teammate? Casey?"

"Me."

Her body stopped mid-dance. "You?"

"Yeah." He shifted his weight. "We're the team."

About a thousand feelings she couldn't identify fought for supremacy. Panic. Horror. Skittishness. But one overriding feeling canceled out all the negatives one by one.

Excitement.

She'd not seen him in proper rescue mode yet, but she had a feeling Zach Murphy was one of those quiet men who rose like a giant when challenged. And she was the one who was going to get to see his hidden talents revealed in all their glory. And then, of course, figure out how to smush all of her sexy feelings into competitive energy, so she could show her brothers she could stand on her own two feet once and for all.

"That's cool," she said, with an air of indifference she definitely didn't feel. She pointed two of her fingers at her own eyes then zapped them at her brother. "You're going *down*, bruh."

Mak laughed and slapped Zach on the back. "Good luck with that."

Zach didn't lurch forward under the weight of the thwack—instead he held his ground. "I'm willing to bet a barbecue dinner we'll win."

Lulu's eyes snapped from Zach to her brother and back again. He was? *Wow.*

She crossed her arms in front of her and gave her brother a *Now who's nervous?* nod.

Mak stuck out his hand, still laughing. "I am more than happy to take that bet. I like my chicken spicy and my burgers pink."

Zach shook his hand and Mak wandered down to the beach, still laughing and shaking his head.

"Wow," Lulu said finally. "That was brave."

Stupid, stupid, stupid, thought Zach. What had he been thinking? Challenging a man mountain who knew the islands as if they were part of his DNA to a search and rescue duel?

No prizes for guessing the answer to that one.

He'd wanted to impress Lulu.

The way she'd looked at him... The way she'd

felt as she'd thrown her arms around him when she'd found out she was on the team… It had been like being hugged by an energy bomb. A surprisingly cuddly energy bomb. A surprisingly sexy energy bomb.

He hadn't missed the way her breasts had pressed against his chest. How perfectly her head had tucked beneath his chin. Her cheeks had pinked when, for a nanosecond, she'd looked up at him, and there had been nothing but sheer joy in her eyes.

So, despite every silent vow he'd made not to cross into the land of romance ever again, he'd found himself crossing it. Like a lovestruck knight intent on jousting for his lady's honor. Only this time the lady in question would be wearing a high-vis vest, a safety harness and belaying down the side of a cliff. She didn't need her honor saved. She needed it championed. And something he'd never before tapped into made him want to be the man who did just that.

A whistle sounded down at the beach.

"We'd better get down there." Lulu held out her hand for Harry, still taking little skippy hops of excitement, broken up by the odd victory swing of her shoulders and hips. "We're gonna beat my big brother!" she sang as she guided them down to where a dark-haired woman was beckoning everyone to gather in front of a row of wetsuits and surfboards.

"That's Chantal," Lulu whispered. "She teaches surfing, but her day job is lifeguard."

Something about the way she said the word *lifeguard* resonated with Zach. It was the same way he said *fireman* or *EMT*. Respect and humility mixed in with the complicated mess of emotions that went with really knowing the job—knowing the people who sometimes lost their lives because of it.

He wondered...

He scrubbed his head as too many memories of shouldering coffins leaped to the fore. He'd lost more colleagues than he cared to mention. He'd not seen what his father had, but he'd definitely offered his condolences more than anyone should have to.

He clocked up another silent notch for Lulu. She had no doubt lost people, too. She wasn't the type to get preachy, or parade around her life experiences to get respect. She wanted to gain it the old-fashioned way. By earning it.

When the safety talk had finished, and they'd

zipped Harry up into a light wetsuit, Lulu looked at Zach but held her hand out to Harry. "This is where I take over. Is that cool?"

"Absolutely."

It was. But it didn't mean he wasn't nervous.

Twenty minutes later he had absorbed the fact that his concerns had been for nothing. Everything that had set him on edge about Lulu that first day they'd met—her air of recklessness, her need to win rather than be right, a daredevilry that left health and safety in the wind—had proved to be groundless worries.

Her work ethic should have resolved his concerns over the past few weeks, because in fairness it was flawless, but whatever it was that was sparking between them had kept him on edge.

He hadn't wanted to put a name to it, but now, seeing her coax his son into standing up on a surfboard on an actual wave, he knew what it was he'd been trying to deny. Attraction. It was a raw, untethered, grab-your-guts-and-won't-let-you-go type of attraction. And it scared the hell out of him.

It was completely different from what he'd shared with his ex. This felt bigger, somehow. More powerful. Impossible to walk away from.

Like she was made of nickel and he was made of iron. Repelling and attracting one another in equal measure.

It wasn't even purely carnal. Not just about her slick of black hair trained into a thick plait down the center of her spine. Or her amber eyes, flashing with hints of copper whenever their eyes met. Or the curve of her hips as they swept into her thighs. Well…they all helped. But it was the smile on his son's face that he'd thank her for forever. His carefree laugh. The ease with which she showed him what was possible rather than, like his ex had, what wasn't.

The memories stung like venom. The pain was deep and long-lasting. But today, here on the beach, watching Lulu and his son swimming and surfing and, yes, occasionally falling into the sea, he felt a peace he hadn't felt in actual years.

He closed his eyes and let himself enjoy the sensation of trusting someone other than his parents with his son's happiness. It gave him access to a hundred other things he hadn't given himself time or permission for. Feeling the heat of the sun on his skin. Acknowledging the rhythmic cadence of the ocean. The soft whir of wind among the palm fronds.

He'd spent so much time thinking about what he didn't have these past few years. This was the first time in a long time that he'd sat back and felt grateful for what he had.

A gorgeous boy.

Loving parents.

A cool, slightly ramshackle house on the beach.

A job.

A beautiful colleague who drove him to the edge of reason...

He blinked his eyes open when he felt water dripping on him. "Hey!"

Lulu stood above him, her pitch-black hair haloed by the sun behind her. Her expression was unreadable.

His son threw himself into his lap, charged with energy and pride, asking over and over again if he had seen him up on the surfboard.

"I did, Harry. You were amazing."

The comment was meant for his son, but somehow Zach's eyes connected with Lulu when he said it. Her smile wavered for a second. She looked out at the ocean, then back at him, her fingers toying with the central zip of her short wetsuit. It took every ounce of strength Zach possessed to keep his eyes on hers and not dip them down to that sweet spot where her breasts arced away from her breastbone.

"*You* wouldn't want to go for a ride, would you?" Lulu asked.

Not what he'd been expecting. "What? With you?"

"No, with my brother," she said, with a roll of her eyes. "Yeah, with me."

He hesitated.

"Forget it." She turned away, as if to go.

"No, I—wait." He stepped toward her and caught her hand in his, scrabbling to form an actual sentence that was made up of real-life words, and short-circuiting because of the electricity buzzing between them, between their hands.

"Honestly..." She shook her head. "It was a stupid idea. It's hard for two adults to be on the same board together, anyway. There's..." Her eyes flicked to his, then dropped to his chest, his hips, his legs, and moved back up again. "There's a lot of contact."

"Dad, look!"

Lulu and Zach followed Harry's finger, which was pointing out to the ocean. There, in the center of the sea of surfers, was Lulu's brother, holding Chantal up with one hand as she arced into a variety of circus-style poses while he effortlessly surfed the pair of them onto the shore, before setting her down as if she were made of fairy dust.

Lulu looked back at Zach and deadpanned, "I'm not sure I have the upper body strength to achieve quite that level of finesse if we were to do the same."

Their eyes locked. The wattage between them ramped up to something that hadn't been invented yet. And there it was again. That magnetic hunger to find out exactly what she felt like. To see how the soft, honeyed surface of her skin would respond to the rough whorls on his fingertips. To his lips.

Standing this close to her, he felt their differences keenly. He was all steel and cement and honking horns, while she was golden sand, soft breezes and rivulets of water shifting along a deep green palm frond. And yet something told him that right at the very center of her heart, of her mind—where it *mattered*—they were made from the same mold. With strong moral compasses. A built-in, unshakable conviction to serve their communities. A belief that everyone should be treated fairly and with kindness, no matter what package they came in.

"Dad?" Harry grabbed his hand and gave him a pleading look. "Can we do this again, please? Tomorrow?"

"Oh…" He faltered. "I think Lulu said it was only once a month…"

"I'll take you out, squirt," Lulu said over him. "If your dad's cool with it, we could practice at Turtle Hideaway."

"That'd be great."

Zach thanked her, trying to give Harry's head a scrub but missing, because his son was too busy jumping up and down. Lulu joined him for his happy dance—which was just as well, because he was finding it hard not to betray the sucker punch of emotion the offer had elicited in him.

She wouldn't know about the number of times Harry had asked his mother to go to the zoo, the park, the playground, only to receive a cringe and a paltry excuse as to why they couldn't go.

Christina's response to having a disabled son had been gutting. It was as if she'd expected her child to be an accessory to her almost unnatural beauty. But when two years of tests had revealed that their son definitely had cerebral palsy, a coldness had fallen in her—like a sheet of ice between her world and theirs.

It had been impossible to believe that she would reject both her son and then, as part of the fall-out, him. But the lure of her career, world travel and being surrounded by nothing but beauty had trumped the vows they'd taken, the life they'd promised to share together, the son they'd sworn to protect. So when they'd separated three years ago and then divorced he had dragged about a hundred chains around his heart and locked it up tight. That sort of risk was never worth taking again.

"I do have one condition," Lulu said, aiming her comment at Zach.

"Name it," he said.

"You and me." She pointed at him, then at herself. "We train. Hard. And then we kick ass at the games." She winced an apology at Harry. "Sorry, bud. I wasn't meant to say ass."

Harry giggled.

Zach waved the apology away. Harry had heard worse. Much worse. Funny how he'd never realized how cruel children and parents could be until he'd started taking Harry to school. He'd caught the tag end of taunts and teasing from the kids, the sidelong glances from the parents and the distance they tried to keep between their children and his, as if Harry's condition was infectious.

Lulu pulled Harry in for a hug. "So? What do you think? Surfing lessons for this little dude in exchange for a bit of hardcore training?"

"Sounds reasonable. But why do you want to win the games so much? We're small fry compared to the teams we're going up against."

From her change of expression and the instant rush of cool air sweeping between them Zach knew he'd done a massive *open mouth, insert foot*.

"Oh? Is that what you think?" Lulu was tapping her bare foot on the sand the way an interrogator might slap a leather baton in their hand. With barely controlled rage. "That we're small fry? That there's no point in trying?"

"No!" he protested. And honestly he didn't. "I don't. It's just that it's our first year in the games, and we've been chosen for optics more than ability—"

"Hold up!" she cut in, holding her hand out to stop him, as if she needed a moment to digest what he'd just said. She turned to Harry and pointed him a bit farther down the beach, to a couple of enormous cool boxes being manned by volunteers. "Hey, bud. Why don't you go grab some bottles of water, yeah? I think your father here is getting a bit of heatstroke." When he'd gone, she turned back to Zach and with barely concealed disgust said, "How did you even get hired if that's how little you think of us?"

"No! I misspoke. I don't think poorly of you or the team. I'm sure we have as much of a chance of winning as any of the others."

He caught a glimpse of Makoa, picking up two little kids, one under each arm, as if they were beach towels. *Oh, God. They didn't stand a chance.*

Lulu, catching the scene, spat back, "You said we were chosen for optics. So…what? We tick all the right boxes? Ethnic woman? Big, sexy, strong fireman? Is this a photo-op or a competition?"

He goldfished for a minute, stuck on the part where she'd called him a "sexy, strong fireman."

She dug her weight into her heels. "You know, when you came along I thought you were a jerk. A highly qualified, talented jerk. Turns out only one of the three was right."

He had to fix this. Fast. "I *am* highly qualified."

Despite her obvious ire, she sniggered. "But not very optimistic."

He sucked in a sharp breath and held up his hands. "You've got me there. And *that's* why I think they put us together."

"Why? Because I'm a dreamer and you're an optics-only guy?"

"No. Because you see options where I don't. And..." He batted round in his frazzled brain for something smart to say. "And I can lift more stuff."

She sniggered again. "*Pfft.* You think you're strong?"

The atmosphere between them shifted, crackling with a whole new breed of tension. The kind that made him want to close the distance between them. So he did.

"Oh, I *know* I'm strong." He was close to her. Close enough that she had to tip that feisty little chin of hers up to meet his gaze.

"How strong?" she asked, in a voice that demanded proof.

"This strong."

Before he could think better of it, he reached out, picked her up, threw her over his shoulder and ran to the sea, gratified to hear her screams of protest turning into laughter. A lot of laughter.

He ran into the surf, deeper and deeper, until a wave slammed against his thighs and the two of them fell into the ocean, her body sliding down his chest, his arms wrapping round her waist to keep her above water, her hands lacing round his neck. When the wave retreated he was still holding her. The water dappled her skin like dewdrops. Their faces weren't even a handful of inches apart, and their bodies were pressed together as if their lives depended upon it...

"Is that all you two got?"

Mak appeared, towering above them, hands extended to pull them both up, the tropical water sloshing round his immovable body as if he were made of granite. He fixed Zach with an intense and highly effective warning glance to get his hands off his little sister. *Immediately.*

Once he'd pulled them up, Mak gave Zach a proper thwack on the back as he chuckled. "You're going to have to prepare yourselves for an epic defeat."

Zach stood back, feigning a devil-may-care attitude he definitely didn't feel. *Hands off Lulu.* That was the unspoken part of that warning.

Message received. Loud and clear.

He glanced at Lulu. Her eyes were lowered to half-mast, her arms were crossed, and she was clearly mortified by her brother's thinly veiled threat.

When she looked up and met his gaze he caught a glimpse of something in her expression that sent a shot of warmth straight through to his heart.

Hope.

He stuck out his hand and did his best not to crumble when Makoa crushed it in his own enormous, meaty paw.

"Game on," he said, then forced himself to lower his voice an octave. "Game on."

CHAPTER SEVEN

LULU HANDED ZACH a carabiner. "Did you know your name means Sea Warrior?"

He snorted and took the metal loop, pushing the rope against the spring-loaded clasp before twisting it into a snug knot. "What? Have you been stalking me on the internet?"

It was a joke, but from Lulu's guilty expression, he saw that was precisely what she'd been doing.

"No," she snapped, handing him another. "I was looking up nicknames for Harry, and as I was at it I thought I'd look up some good nicknames for us. You know… For the competition."

"Sea Warrior, eh?"

She nodded, tempering the quick flare of defensiveness that had clouded her expression.

Zach grinned. "You tell me I'm a sea warrior just before I'm about to throw myself off the side of a mountain?"

They looked at the sheer drop they were just about to rappel down.

Lulu smirked. "I would've thought the King of Health and Safety wouldn't dream of describing his unparalleled rappelling efforts as 'throwing himself off the side of a mountain.'"

"Good point," he conceded with a smile—one he'd grown used to wearing whenever he was with Lulu.

Ever since he'd had virtually every bone in his hand pulverized into sand by her brother, he'd felt as if he and Lulu were joined in a silent truce. One in which they were united in their mission to show both the Hawaiian Coast Guard and the Ocean Safety Team that their little "ramshackle crew of misfits" were the best in the business.

It didn't mean they were a hundred percent simpatico. There were still a few knots and kinks to smooth out in their teamwork—wanting to rip her clothes off being top of the list.

He wasn't a vain man, but he couldn't help thinking she felt the same way. But something told him that if they broke the seal on whatever it was that was simmering between them there would be no turning back—and Lulu Kahale was not a woman he wanted to disappoint.

Despite his best efforts, his feelings for her were growing, no matter how "chalk and cheese" they appeared on paper.

He ran his life by the rule book.

She swore blind that it was critical to know when to go rogue.

He dialed back the risk in his life.

She liked nothing more than to push the limits.

And yet...the more he got to know her, the more he felt they had more in common than initially met the eye.

She'd not spelled it out, but it was clear her parents hadn't been with her for some time, and she'd pretty much been raised by five very protective older brothers. Anyone who fell in love with Lulu would have to have Superman-like resolve. He didn't know if he had that amount of love to give. And laying down a book of rules as thick as the complete works of Shakespeare, most of which would be about Harry, would send most women running for the hills.

Lulu likes a challenge...

And, of course, there was the undeniable fact that in the love stakes Harry was utterly smitten. His son introduced Lulu to everyone as his best friend, and he counted down the days, hours and minutes until their surf lessons, which were pretty much every day after school now.

School. Snack. Surf lesson. A bit of larking around with the sea turtles.

Then Harry would go in to shower and help Zach's mom make dinner, while he and Lulu had an hour's training session on the beach.

Pushing enormous tires up and over in the wet sand. Climbing palm trees. Tying knots. Untying knots. Swimming out to the reef as fast as they could. Alternating turns in dragging one another back to the shore.

Pretending like hell that being close to her didn't turn him on more than he'd ever been turned on in his life...

So, yeah. Being at the top of this rappelling rope felt a lot like his life had felt these past couple of weeks. Like riding a yo-yo that went in only one direction.

He eased himself off the edge, both hands on the rope as he leaned back and found the sweet spot where the ropes and harnesses took his weight. His phone rang. They both looked at it, wedged into his top breast pocket.

"Want me to get that?" she asked.

He could get it. Rejigger his position so that

he was holding the ropes with one hand. But the naughty devil he hadn't realized was perched on his shoulder had other ideas.

"Could you?"

She knelt down and pinched it between her fingers. The heat of her hand seared through the fabric of his shirt as she withdrew the phone. Their eyes met. Was she taking her time with this? Enjoying their proximity as much as he was? Or was she sharing the torture of indecision? Did they look at what this was humming between them or didn't they?

His phone rang again and she pushed herself back and up, her mixed scent of vanilla and frangipani surrounding him in a little cloud of Lulu that retreated as quickly as she did.

"Murphy's phone," she said, using her self-appointed "grown-up" voice. She listened for a second, then her eyes snapped to his, her body growing taut as if poised on a starting line.

"What?" he asked, already pulling himself back up and over the edge.

She hung up the call and handed the phone to him. "Hiker hasn't been seen in three days. Julia Thompson. Her husband called it in. He was searching for her himself, but lost his bearings. Some smoke was spotted farther up along this trail. Casey's waiting with Stewart. They're going to head over in the chopper if you and I find her."

"*When* you and I find her," Zach corrected, moving back from the ravine edge.

She smiled at him and made an approving noise. "I see some of my positivity is rubbing off on you."

"And some of my cautiousness is wearing off on *you*," he said, his brow furrowing as he realized it might actually be true.

He wasn't so sure he liked that. There was something unfettered and untamed about her that he never wanted to see trapped in a vise of strict regulations.

"Nah…" Lulu swiped at the air between them. "Don't you worry 'bout that, Mr. Rules and Regs. I'm sure there'll always be some fault you see in me to improve upon."

"I doubt that," he said, before he could stop himself.

Her eyes locked with his. Something charged and intimate exploded in the space between them.

"We'd better get going," she whispered, before the moment could fully take hold.

The two of them swiftly moved into a synchronized rhythm he hadn't realized they shared. Pulling in the ropes. Coiling them. Putting everything back in its exact place in the run bags. It spoke of the hours of training they'd put in together, but also nodded at something deeper. Something innate. A shared understanding that came with a heightened awareness of each other.

Zach was going to have to find a way to check it. He hadn't moved here to fall in love. He'd moved here to give his son a solid foundation upon which to build his life. He would force himself to remember the emotional scars his marriage had left.

"You okay?"

Lulu was looking up at him as he shouldered his pack.

"Yeah, why?"

"You look... I don't know... You don't look like you're in a good place to go out on a rescue hike."

"I'm good," he assured her. "C'mon. Let's go."

Lulu set off at her usual brisk pace. Five enormous brothers setting the pace throughout her childhood had pretty much meant running before she could walk. Which some people—like Zach, for instance—might say was her main problem. Racing headlong into situations before she'd drawn up the diagram. Calculated all the risks.

How could she explain to them that there was something in her, something innate, that she felt kept her safe? Privately, she thought it was her mother. A guardian angel watching out over her only daughter. But on a practical level she'd grown up with parents who had set the tone for a life of pushing limits. They'd been lifeguards. They'd known the ocean as well as themselves. Well… Almost as well.

They would never know if their mother had realized how bad the surf was when she'd grabbed her board and gone out looking for a tourist who'd decided surfing was a good idea well after the warning flags had been raised. What they did know was that their father had definitely known how bad it was and he'd gone out, anyway.

He'd always said life wouldn't be worth living if it didn't have their mother in it. Turned out he'd meant it literally.

Their deaths had irrevocably changed them. Her brothers all had jobs that pushed the limits— navy SEAL, volcanologist, bodyguard, stuntman, and, of course, Mak—her rival over at Ocean Safety. Even so, they all liked the firm set of rules and regulations that came with their jobs. But Lulu… She liked the fact that her crew went that one step beyond. Pushed harder. Further.

Zach had definitely bristled when he'd first met her, but now… Up until about thirty seconds ago she would've put money on the fact that he *liked* that about her.

But something had happened between them back there, and whatever it was had made the atmosphere between them awkward. First-day awkward. Awkward like back when they hadn't liked each other very much.

A desperate longing to revert to the strangely flirty, competitive, excited-to-see-each-other vibe that had been humming between them gripped her. She microscopically analyzed the exchange.

She'd said something about him finding fault with her…

He'd said he didn't think he could…

That comment had pulled them both up short, instigating another one of those magic moments they'd been sharing with increasing frequency.

Those moments when their eyes connected and the rest of the world seemed to fade away, when their bodies—hers, anyway—buzzed with an energy that felt anything but earthbound.

Then they'd kind of leaned toward each other.

No. That wasn't right. It had been as if they were being *pulled* toward one another by an invisible force, proactively begging them to kiss. She might have even closed her eyes.

And then it had ended.

He'd got up, they'd sorted the gear, and from the look on his face something had happened in that head of his that had turned their magic moment into a dark one.

She couldn't think what it could be apart from the almost-kiss.

Equal rushes of shame and anger twisted in her gut. Was she that horrendous an option?

A vulnerability she rarely let herself acknowledge exploded inside her. Zach was a class-A example of the type of man she had promised herself she would never, ever fall for. An uptight, regulations-mad mainlander. And yet none of it seemed to matter. This wasn't just a crush anymore. She genuinely liked him. Respected him. She also liked his kid.

If he had no plans on returning her feelings, she was going to have to find a way to rein hers in quick smart.

And then another thought occurred.

Makoa.

Her brother had quite the track record in meddling in her ever-diminishing private life. Maybe he'd got to Zach. Warned him off.

Another twist of white-hot frustration wrenched her stomach into a hot, tangled mess.

Her brothers didn't understand boundaries. They had no problem pulling unsuspecting suitors to one side for a "quiet word" that sent them running for the hills—or, as was more often the case, the airport. Hence the no-mainlanders rule.

But Zach didn't seem like someone who would be intimidated by her brother. He'd worked for the New York City Fire Department, for heaven's sake. She'd seen the calendars. Muscular hunks were a dime a dozen over there.

So what was it, then?

They hiked in silence.

An unbearable one.

Unable to take it anymore, she reeled on him. His body slammed into hers, the impact forcing out the question running over and over in her mind.

"What?" she demanded. "What's wrong with me?"

They had grabbed on to one another for balance. Her fingers were pressing into the musculature of his lower back. Or were they? *Oh, no.* That wasn't his back. She'd just grabbed his butt.

His arms were wrapped around her entire body, as if he were protecting her from an avalanche. It was an instinctive move. One that had to mean he felt *something* for her. Didn't it?

She chanced a look up into his face.

Her question hung in what little space was left between them.

"Nothing," he whispered.

Again, that taut, hypnotic energy wrapped around the pair of them like a thick, opulent, tingle-inducing ribbon. Their breaths came deep and charged. His eyes darkened to a rich sapphire blue and shone with a brightness she'd not seen in them before. Before a single, helpful thought could find its way into Lulu's brain, he was lowering his mouth to hers. His touch was soft at first. Tentative. But when he felt she was returning his kisses they grew more heated. Hungry.

Her mouth was exploring his. His lips were teasing and taunting, then rewarding her for her curiosity. Her desire. She wasn't in charge of her body anymore. It had a mind of its own. As their kisses intensified she was vaguely aware that she was arching her chest into his, raising up on her tiptoes the better to pull his lower lip slowly, achingly against her teeth.

Her hips fitted perfectly between his. There was no doubt that his body had lost control as much as hers had. Her limbs twitched with the desire to regroup, find new handholds. To climb him like a tree, wrap her legs round his hips and press her mouth to his as if their kisses would save the world.

And then she heard the helicopter.

Her brain was instantly yanked back to reality. *What the actual hell?* She was making out with her boss when they were supposed to be rescuing someone.

This was why "office" romances were verboten. This was also why there was always that added layer of frisson whenever she was with him. It was a relationship that had death knells tolling around it before it had even begun.

She stumbled back a few steps, instantly feeling cold in every part of her body that had been touched by his. "We should get on," she managed, through short, sharp exhalations.

"Yeah."

Zach's voice was rough. Not angry rough. Heated rough. As if they'd just been caught in a tornado, whisked up high enough to catch a glimpse of whatever it was on the other side of the rainbow, then unceremoniously dropped straight back down to earth again.

Pounding his fists into his own head wasn't an option. Nor was ripping up his contract. Nor was yanking his heart out of his chest and flinging it off the edge of the cliff.

Finding this hiker and getting her to safety was. Quickly followed by opening up his laptop, applying for a new job and booking a one-way flight to...

Where?

He couldn't move every time something happened that wasn't part of the plan.

Couldn't break up with it.

Couldn't divorce it.

Couldn't sugarcoat it with the godsend that Grandma and Grandpa would be there to take up the slack where Mommy had once been.

The pragmatics of his "well-laid plan" seemed insignificant now.

From the moment he'd met her, Zach had known right down to his very cell structure that falling for Lulu Kahale was out of the question. And yet he'd been the one to instigate it. The one who'd crossed the line he'd thought he'd drawn in the sand.

What on God's green earth had he been thinking?

Nothing. Obviously. He'd let his more primitive instincts take over when he should've pushed them off the side of this ravine they were now edging along.

He picked up the pace, curling his hands into fists, pumping them ahead of him as if trying to build up enough speed to take off and fly. Unspent energy, trying to find something useful to do with itself.

It was a real kick in the teeth to have been put in his place by the job. The one thing he prioritized after his son. Those were the two things that had kept him upright while he'd come to terms with the fact that his wife didn't want to parent their disabled child.

He let a stream of silent curse words loose in his brain to try to get his body to forget how good Lulu had felt in his arms. Pressed up against him. Matching the energy of his kisses as if she'd been waiting a lifetime for just that moment.

"Hey." Lulu stopped and pointed a hundred meters ahead toward the ravine.

He saw it in an instant. Smoke.

They began to jog, Lulu pulling out her phone and calling the station to give Stewart the coordinates.

A weak-voiced "Help…" bounced up the ravine walls.

Swiftly they pulled out their rappelling gear. Zach looked at Lulu. One of them had to stay up top to signal to the helicopter—the other would go down and perform as much first aid as possible.

"You go," she said.

"You sure?" Even after only a few weeks, he knew she would've happily jumped into the harness and onto the end of the rope line every single time.

"I'm sure."

The subtext of the decision was coming through loud and clear. *You're the boss. We shouldn't have kissed. Now, go.*

He swiftly lowered himself down the edge of the ravine into the jungle canopy. The hiker was only a few meters away from the spot where he touched down.

He gave a shout to Lulu that this was the spot, unclipped his harness and ran over to her. "I'm Zach. I'm guessing you're Julia?"

She was in obvious pain. Her ankle, just visible above her hiking boot, was a myriad of purples and blues.

She nodded. "Good guess. Did…" her voice faltered "…did my husband tell you I was missing?"

Zach nodded.

Her features tightened as if she was going to cry. She pointed at her right foot. "I didn't take my boot off because I thought if anything was sticking out I didn't want to see it." She winced as she readjusted her feet on the ground.

"That was smart. Compound fractures need to be kept as stabilized as possible, but I think you'd know if you had a break that bad." He knelt down beside her and gave her a quick scan. A few cuts and bruises. Dirt streaks on her face, arms and legs. Quite a few mosquito bites. "They'll take a proper look at that ankle in the hospital, but it looks like a long hot bath in some Epsom salts would be the best medicine for the rest of you."

"No!" She protested with a feeble laugh. "No hot baths. No hot anything. I'm desperate to be in a room with aircon. If you could put me in a room with a snowman I'd be over the moon."

Zach smiled, pleased she still had enough spirit to make lame jokes.

He unhooked his first aid kit from his shoulders and tugged out a bottle of water. "Here. You must be thirsty. Slow, steady sips. Don't gulp it."

She gave another tired, weak laugh. "That's the one thing I have managed to do. Drink lots of water." She nodded at a nearby stream. "I wasn't sure if it would be safe, but after a few hours in the heat I didn't really care."

He nodded, quickly taking note of her tiny day pack and the small fire she'd managed to build. She'd be hungry, too. He pulled an energy bar out of his backpack and, again, cautioned her to eat it slowly.

It had been three days since she'd disappeared.

He was about to ask why it had taken her so long to build the fire when he pulled himself up short, wondering what Lulu would've done if she was in his shoes.

Focus on the positive, fix what you can, then find the facts.

"Good thing you brought matches," he said.

Her smile faltered. "Lighter, actually. It's the reason why I'm in this mess."

He arced an eyebrow.

"I suppose it's also the reason you found me." She made a small sobbing noise and a solitary tear trickled down her cheek before she covered her face with her hands and explained, "Even when he's angry with me he's always there, looking after me."

"Who?"

Zach looked up at a sharp noise and saw that Lulu had fired the flare gun for Stewart.

"Not long now," he said, pointing at the sky, where the helicopter could be heard approaching. He tugged a couple of instant ice packs out of his first aid kit to strap on to her ankle.

Absorbed in the story she had to tell, Julia began to speak as if her life depended upon it. "My husband and I were on a hike. We had a fight about his smoking. He got so angry he pulled out his cigarettes and his lighter, saying I made him so stressed he had to smoke. So I grabbed them and threw them into the ravine. But the lighter was his dad's, you see. Engraved and everything. I've never seen him so angry."

The words continued in a torrent.

"He stormed off. I stayed where I was for a while, certain he'd come back, but after an hour or so I figured he'd gone back to the hotel. So I thought, *I know! I'll find the lighter and take it to him, and we'll make up, and this won't be the worst vacation of our lives after all!* I love him so much… I just hate his smoking. But after one night in the jungle on my own I realized making a stand about something that really is his choice isn't worth living without him, you know? I just couldn't imagine a life without—"

Emotion strangled the rest of her sentence into nonexistence.

"Hey." Zach gave her hand a squeeze. "We've got you now. *And* you found the lighter. It helped us find you. That's got to be a sign that things will be all right, doesn't it?"

She nodded. "I hope so."

Zach gave her hand another squeeze, then excused himself to go and help as the helicopter approached, hovered overhead, then lowered the static stretcher, which Lulu jumped on from the hiking path above.

When their eyes connected he saw questions in them. Doubts. Seeds of insecurity he knew he'd sown because of his lug-headed response to having kissed her.

They loaded Julia onto the stretcher, and after Zach volunteered to hike out with the gear, Lulu silently agreed to ride in the chopper with her.

Come to think of it, she'd barely said a word since she'd joined them. He didn't like seeing her this way. And he liked it less that her silence was his fault.

"I'll see you at the hospital, yeah?" he said before they began their ascent.

She gave him a sharp look. "I don't know. Will you?"

The question remained unanswered as Lulu gave the signal to pull them up.

Zach nodded at Julia, his mind still whirring on the fight she'd had with her husband over something that on the surface seemed small, but really was enormous. She wanted him to live a happy, healthy life. With her.

Zach wanted to live a happy, healthy life, too. A safe, secure, predictable life. It seemed the wisest option.

His eyes followed Lulu as she was pulled up and beyond the jungle canopy, and he thought of how she put herself in the face of danger every single day but came out unscathed.

He'd never allowed room for the possibility that he could love someone again. Least of all someone who did search and rescue. It wasn't just him he was looking after. It was his son.

An image flashed through his mind's eye of Harry and Lulu on the surfboard. Harry's slight, little-boy body being held upright on the board as he and Lulu caught a wave. His son's smile bigger than he'd ever seen it before at his achievement.

Would seeing that smile on a regular basis be worth risking his heart?

He zipped up his run bag, shouldered it, and began to hike. He didn't know. He didn't know anything anymore except that he and Lulu were going to be spending three entire days together on the Big Island, competing in those blasted games. The proximity would make or break them. Give them answers to the questions he was too damn scared to ask.

He looked up at the sky and caught a glimpse of the retreating helicopter.

One foot in front of the other, he told himself. That was how he'd climbed out of the dark hole he'd fallen into during the breakdown of his marriage, and eventually he'd made it to the top. He hadn't expected to find himself at the bottom all over again for the completely opposite reason. He'd thought falling for someone was supposed to feel good.

He caught himself up short. Was he falling for her?

He shook his head. Nope. He already had. Now he'd hit the crossroads where he had to figure out whether or not to do anything about it.

CHAPTER EIGHT

"WATER AND SUNBLOCK," Lulu said sternly to the little girl.

She pouted.

Her mother gave an exasperated sigh. "I've been telling her the only way to stop the freckles is to wear sunblock!"

Lulu gave the mother a quick scan, noted her immaculate make-up, nails and generally stylish aesthetic. Her little girl had almost succumbed to heatstroke and was only a couple of shades of red away from a dangerous sunburn.

She decided common sense and threats of skin cancer weren't going to work, so she tried another tack. "Are you cool with face painting?"

The mother shrugged, a bit confused, so Lulu asked the little girl what her favorite animal was.

"A cat!" she said, a big smile replacing the pout.

"Cool. Cats..."

Lulu grinned, then grabbed a couple of different tubes of colored sunblock. She was more of a dolphin person herself…but to each their own. She could work with a cat. Which kind of rhymed with Zach. Which instantly made a wash of guilt pour into her as she remembered the multiple texts she'd ignored from him after she'd taken herself off shift, claiming she was due vacation time, and then promptly signed up for some shifts with the ambulance crew and about a million training hours at the gym.

All time they could've spent training for the games.

Together.

Like a proper team.

Today's ambulance posting was at Waikiki Beach—the most popular expanse of surf and sand on the island.

She drew for a bit—a few whiskers, a splotch of a nose and, of course, some large freckles to cover the real ones—then leaned back and grinned. "Wanna see?"

The little girl clapped her hands. "Yes, please!"

Lulu dug her phone out of her pocket, took a picture, then showed the girl—who cooed at herself in the way only little girls could. With undiluted delight.

The mother gave Lulu a grateful smile of thanks, then the two of them padded off, hand in hand, the little girl skipping a bit now that she was rehydrated, and gabbling away about how much she loved it here.

Watching the two of them scraped against something in Lulu's heart she rarely let herself acknowledge. She'd never really wanted to have a baby. It was a tie that bound you to another human being in a way that freaked her right out. To two humans, actually. The father. The child itself.

How her parents had apportioned their hearts out to six children *and* each other boggled her mind.

The thought caught her up sharp.

The portions hadn't been equal.

The bonds of marital love were what had compelled her father to jump on his surfboard to go and find her mother, even though he had known two lives might be lost that day. From Lulu's perspective, it was indelible proof that loving someone meant making choices.

Who was worth living for and who was worth dying for?

It was a lose-lose tug of war she'd never been

able to figure out when it came to her personal life, and most likely the thing that had always compelled her to keep her relationships short and sweet. Which did beg the question: Why have them at all?

Because deep down you know you want it, knucklehead. You know you want to love that hard. That big. That generously.

She forced herself to dial back the deep thoughts and remember what had pulled her down this rabbit hole in the first place.

Babies. That was it. Babies…

A little shudder swept through her, then stalled…

Primary school kids…teens…her ever-increasing gaggle of nieces and nephews… She couldn't get enough of them. Instead of decreasing the amount of love she had, each new arrival, whenever one appeared, opened up a fresh expanse of love she hadn't realized she could tap into. And it wasn't just her nieces and nephews. It was the kids down at the Superstars Surf Club. Harry…

The tug of longing turned into a tight, achy knot. Avoiding Zach hadn't meant neglecting Harry. She'd continued to teach him to surf. He shouldn't be penalized just because his dad had a fiercely grabbable ass and desperately kiss-able lips.

She closed her eyes as the knot in her stomach turned molten and started swirling around inside her. She could even smell him. That citrusy man scent that... Wait a minute...

She blinked her eyes open. If stomachs could plummet and flutter all at the same time, that was what hers was doing.

"Hey," Zach said, giving her a hip-height wave.

Hips she had fit into as if they were Lego pieces, born to nestle together, snug and perfect.

She swallowed and tried to look as if her insides weren't throwing themselves a party. "Hey, yourself."

Nice one, Lulu. Way to show him you aren't re-enacting your teenage how-to-snag-a-guy skills.

Zach cleared his throat, his body language shifting from wary to defensive. "Forgive me for being a bit slow on the uptake, but is this whole taking a vacation to work another job your way of saying you don't want to represent the OST at the games?"

Her entire body leaped to attention. "No. Absolutely not."

He didn't move, but she was pretty sure his

eyes had turned a warmer shade of blue. "Okay. Well, in that case, you *are* aware we have to leave for the Big Island tonight, right?"

"Yes," she scoffed.

Duh. She knew the start date of the games like she knew the Fourth of July. It was one of those dates branded into her annual calendar. Which day, which island, which resort...

All of a sudden her brain was flooded with images of the resort where they'd be staying...the cocktails she'd have to resist drinking to stay out of the bed where Zach would be sleeping. And Zach must be having a similar sort of mental slideshow, because the already humid air had turned about as thick and sultry as it could without actually plunging the two of them into one of Hawaii's sudden downpours.

"How's Harry?" she asked.

"Good." Zach nodded. "Still loving his surf lessons, so... Thanks for keeping your word about that."

A protest caught in her throat, but she caught it just in time. She'd told Zach she'd train with him and she hadn't, so she deserved that jibe. Harry, though... She wasn't about to let her mixed-up feelings about his dad get in the way of their relationship. He was just a kid. He didn't deserve to be caught in the crossfire of whatever it was that was happening between them.

"Well…" Zach shifted a pile of sand from one foot to the other. "Shame we've missed out on a week's worth of training."

His tone was impossible to read. Which, of course, made her insanely crazy. She wanted to strangle him and kiss him all at the same time. Scream at him. *How on earth do you think we're ever going to win the games if all I'm thinking about is what you feel like naked?*

And then, to her horror, she realized she'd just said all that in her out-loud voice.

"Hey, bruh." Lulu's colleague for the day, Jason, came round the corner, holding a couple of popsicles. He looked from Zach to Lulu and said, "Shift's over." He handed her one of the frozen treats, then gauged the energy surging between the pair of them. "I would've got another if I'd known you had company."

Lulu took her popsicle, made the introductions and then, to give herself something to do other than go back to her sexy, angry staring contest with Zach, began to eat it.

When she realized Zach was watching her with

something a lot more like lust than disdain, she felt herself coil like a boa constrictor, seeing his desire.

"We're going to the Intra-Island Search and Rescue Games tonight," she said to Jason, and then, to Zach, "What time is the flight?"

"Seven. I can pick you up if you like," he said, his eyes not leaving her mouth as she tried and failed to stop her tongue from swirling round the top of her popsicle as if it were—

The ambulance radio squawked out a report.

"If you two lovebirds will excuse me?" Jason said.

Neither of them acknowledged the comment. They weren't lovebirds. They were lust monsters. One of them in a grotty end-of-shift uniform, one in a disturbingly sexy pair of completely ordinary cargo shorts and an old NYFD T-shirt.

How on earth did he *do* that? Make off-the-rack athleisure wear look as if it demanded attention? Demanded fingers on buttons, on zips, tugging, pulling, getting that waistband off those perfect hips and tugged down until—

"Lulu!" Jason banged on the side of the ambulance. "Someone was playing Tarzan up the road and needs an ambulance. Want some overtime?"

She could barely remember her own name right now, let alone divine if she wanted overtime or not. "Yes..."

"Wanna do a ride along?" Jason asked Zach. "See how the real rescue crews work?"

Lulu whirled on Jason. "Zach worked for Fire and Rescue in New York," she said, far more defensively than she probably should have.

Jason smiled and put out his fist to Zach. "Respect, dude. Things run at a different pace out there. Wanna come along and see how we roll?"

"Sure."

"You two strap yourselves in the back," he said, with a wink to Lulu. "Give you a chance for some alone time."

They did as they were told, each of them buckling into a bench seat with nothing but a stretcher between them. It might have been the entire expanse of the Pacific Ocean or a toothpick. He felt both near and far away. Impossible to have and just as impossible not to.

After what felt like an eternity, but was actually about thirty seconds, Zach broke the silence. "We don't have to do this, you know."

"It's a bit late now!" She held out her hands, pointing out the obvious, then lurched forward as Jason took a sharp turn. Her hands landed on Zach's chest. He wrapped his fingers round her wrists and leaned in, holding her there, close. Too close.

"The games," he said.

She tugged her hands free. "Oh, no. No, no, no, you don't. We are definitely doing those."

Zach flinched, as if scorched by the fire in her pronouncement. "Why? Why're they so important to you?"

"Because it'll prove to my brothers I don't need to be protected. If I don't win these games and prove I have what it takes, they'll never leave me alone!"

There. She'd said it. She needed to prove her strength to her brothers once and for all. Now that Zach had taken her job, her house and her common sense, the games were all she had left.

He studied her in silence, his eyes searching hers in the same way he inspected a patient. Looking for the pain. For the real source of the injury beyond the superficial.

How could she explain what she was going through and not sound insane? How could she tell him that falling in love the way her parents had…the way she was doing with Zach this very second…was the most terrifying thing in the world? Love like theirs meant crossing the line. Paddling out into an ocean you knew could devour you whole.

It was why she pushed so hard. Accepted rescues that might mean possibly never coming back. She wanted to see just how far she could go and still retain control. Only when she'd pushed those limits far enough so that her brothers had to acknowledge her strength, her resilience, could she finally start to allow those other things she wanted in life some oxygen.

"Is that what you really want?" Zach finally asked. "To be left alone?"

It was a loaded question and they both knew it.

If she said yes, she knew he'd come to the games, behave impeccably, give them his all. But he wouldn't have that extra fire, the charged glow he always had when they pulled off some feat or another together.

If she said no…

Her heart strained at the thought of stopping this—whatever it was—before it even had a chance to begin.

"No."

"Well, then," Zach sat back, his eyes sparking

with a determined resolve she'd not seen in them before. "What do you propose we do?"

Zach folded the cocktail napkin into ever-reducing squares, then watched it unfold when he released it. It was a metaphor, he told himself, for earlier this afternoon.

When Lulu hadn't answered his question in the ambulance he'd stayed quiet. He'd offered an extra pair of hands when "Tarzan" had needed his ribs wrapped but refused because it would "totes mess up" his tan line. He'd changed his mind when Zach had started asking Lulu about the dangers of punctured lungs.

He liked how they worked together. How they could each read a patient, pick an angle and go with it after a small shared acknowledgment. Her amber eyes would glow with the love of a challenge, with the rush of adrenaline that came from every rescue, every patient—no matter if it was a lack of sunblock on a toddler or a surfer with a bloodied nose and a concussion after his board had smashed against his face.

He liked her.

Plain and simple.

Probably more.

Definitely more.

But that was a drawbridge he wasn't yet prepared to cross. Not until she figured out what she wanted. He hadn't planned on falling in love, let alone finding himself neck-deep in unrequited love, but something deep in his gut told him this wasn't unrequited. More...undecided. And not because of him.

But he had his son to think about. To prioritize. Forever and always. And if that meant backing away from a girl who made his heart pound against his rib cage every time he saw her so be it.

"Here you go!" Lulu appeared in front of him holding two cocktail glasses shaped like pineapples, one in front of each breast.

He looked away. They were here for the games. Not for him to ogle her breasts.

"Hope you like rum," Lulu said, putting the drink in front of him and taking a rather large gulp of her own. "It's pretty much all a mai tai is made out of."

He took a sip and choked. "Wow!" He drank deeply from his water glass. "You weren't kidding."

Lulu raised one of her eyebrows at him and, her eyes still connected to his, took a long, thirst-quenching drink of her own mai tai. No flinching. No wriggling as the alcohol hit her nervous system. Nothing apart from a tiny quirk at the corner of her mouth as if she'd just given him a test and he'd failed.

Maybe hers was a virgin cocktail.

Zach was about to ask what else was in the drink when a towering figure of a man thundered across the open-air bar.

"It's Mini-Menehune!"

"Oh, Lordy..." Lulu took another large gulp of her drink, shot a quick, "Prepare yourself," to Zach, then jumped up and did a double *shaka*. "Hey, bruh. Howzit?"

She threw a quick glance back at Zach. One that said, *Stand up. Don't let him tower over you.*

He stayed where he was. He'd met plenty of men like Makoa. Physically intimidating, made of machismo, but when push came to shove, if you found the right trigger, made of molten caramel inside. He had a pretty good idea that Lulu was his trigger...so he'd stay where he was.

Makoa, as anticipated, saw that Zach hadn't stood up and, sensing his sister's nerves, crossed to him and put out his hand. "Hey, bruh. Good to see you again."

Tick!

Zach took the hand and shook it. "Nice to see you."

"Ready for the games tonight?"

Zach shook his head, confused. "I thought they didn't start until tomorrow?"

"No, bruh." Makoa unleashed one of his belly-jiggling laughs. "The *proper* games start tomorrow…the *team building* games start tonight."

"Team building?" Lulu's eyebrows arrowed toward her nose.

Makoa swiped an enormous paw in the air. "Aw, you know… It's all of that touchy-feely *If I trust you, we can do anything* sort of stuff."

"Oh, right. I see." Lulu took another, immensely large gulp of her drink and then, with a casual air Zach knew she wasn't owning, asked, "Are there prizes?"

Makoa patted her head, changing his voice so he sounded like a kindergarten teacher. "Yes, my darling little sister. There will be prizes." Then he leaned back and roared with laughter. "Probably the only ones *you'll* be winning this weekend."

Zach bristled on Lulu's behalf. Sibling rivalry was one thing, but he was pretty sure Makoa didn't understand how much these games meant to Lulu. Which killed him. She was smart, beautiful, fun, adventurous, talented and a thousand other things he shouldn't be thinking about if he wanted his feelings to stay anywhere near neutral. The last thing Lulu Kahale needed was a medal hanging round her neck to prove she was worth caring for.

As if sensing his understanding, she shot a glance at him, her amber eyes bright with ambition and a sliver of vulnerability. She rarely gave away her trust. And she was trusting him.

"Wanna join in?" she asked.

"Of course," Zach said, as if not joining had never occurred to him.

He pushed his drink away, then wove his fingers together and stretched them as if preparing for a workout. He silently thanked whatever Hawaiian gods were out there for the excuse not to get tipsy enough to try to kiss Lulu again. He didn't know if that ship had sailed, but he certainly wasn't going to try anything this weekend.

He pushed up and out of his chair and began to jog in place. "I'm ready when you are."

Makoa snorted. "Looks like my little sis is dropping you in it, my man."

"We're up for anything," Zach said, putting out his arm and pulling Lulu to his side, trying his best to ignore the physical satisfaction that came from feeling her nestle in close beneath his arm as she slipped one of her arms round his waist. "Aren't we, Lulu?"

He looked down at her, his entire body getting a full-force injection of pride when he saw her beaming back up at him.

"Totally," she said to him. Then, to her brother, "Bring it on."

An hour later Zach was deeply regretting the whole all-for-one-one-for-all bravura that had propelled him and Lulu up onto a stage with Makoa and his teammate—the last four standing—where they would complete the final trust exercise of the night.

Makoa's colleague—a petite woman, Kiko—was the human form of a firecracker. Fast, charged, and prone to go off when you least expected it. And Makoa was, of course, a mountain of muscle. Immovable if need be and surprisingly nimble when called to action. He'd be tough to beat tomorrow. He'd be tough to beat tonight.

Everyone had thought the very first trust exercise—the one where one partner had to fall into the arms of the other while wearing a blindfold—would finish Kiko because, of course, Makoa was the one chosen to fall into her arms. But she'd performed a circus-like stop-drop-and-roll maneuver that had broken his fall. Not strictly a pillow-soft landing, but...

Here they all were. In the finals.

The crowd, juiced up on mai tais, was whooping and cheering. Makoa and Kiko were obvious favorites because they were known commodities, whereas Zach, a mainlander *haole* and Lulu, the kid sister he was quickly realizing everyone had been forewarned to treat with kid gloves, were not.

As the evening had progressed, he'd gained a genuine understanding of what it must've been like for Lulu growing up in the shadows of her big brothers. He, after all, had only met one. And there were four more of them out there. As such, he'd put his all into the evening, easily allowing himself to unbuckle his tendency not to trust. This was for Lulu.

With each passing challenge the energy exchange between the pair of them had grown more and more fine-tuned. To the point where they'd even managed to gain some of their own cheer-leaders—rescue crews who clearly liked seeing the underdog challenge the reigning champions, as Makoa's team had been for the last ten years.

"Quiet, you lot!" The emcee for the evening—a man with a steel-gray crew cut, who would also be leading events over the weekend—held out his hands to quiet down the whistles and the whooping. "The final event of the night is…" he paused for dramatic effect "…the handcuff challenge!"

The audience erupted with explosive laughter, hoots and hollers.

Zach threw Lulu a look. What the hell was the handcuff challenge?

She shrugged. This was her first time, too. She was as much in the dark as he was.

The emcee explained. The pair of them would be handcuffed together with "team-building cuffs"—whatever they were. It *was* possible to break free, they were told, but only by using the highest level of teamwork and taking onboard hints and suggestions from the audience, who would be split in two. One half for Makoa and Kiko. One half for Zach and Lulu. They'd have five minutes.

It had taken a Herculean effort for Zach not to notice that the few swigs of mai tai Lulu had taken as Dutch courage had made her a bit more...erm...*pliable* in the physicality department. She'd been the one to fall into his arms during the trust exercise. But, rather than doing it the old-fashioned way, she'd somehow twisted and whirled herself in the air so that she'd landed in his arms like a damsel in distress.

Well... A damsel who had then leaped out of his arms and paraded round the stage shouting, "That's how we roll!"

Now they were turned back to back, their wrists bound with some sort of rubbery rope. It wasn't very flexible, and allowed very little room for maneuver. The audience was shouting all sorts of options. Dislocate a shoulder. A thumb. Shred what little dignity they had and give up now.

All options Zach felt it wise to table.

Lulu turned her head away from the crowd, her hair brushing against his cheek as he turned to her. She whispered up to him, "Follow my lead, okay? I've got this."

He gave a quick affirmative noise, hoping she knew what she was talking about. Spending the rest of the evening tied to Lulu, who was already wriggling against his butt like a supercharged sexy Easter bunny, was going to be his biggest challenge yet. The last thing he needed was to get a hard-on in front of Hawaii's finest.

Mind over matter, he told himself on a loop. *Mind over matter.*

"Crouch down," Lulu said. "I'm going to have to climb over you."

"What?"

"Or maybe slip under you," she said, already lowering herself down so that he had no choice but to follow. "Not sure yet."

He felt her body press hard against his, then pull away. With a quick grunt and a tug on his hands, he felt Lulu do something like a somersault in the limited space between them. Their bound wrists were pressing into her chest…his back was still toward her. If he had the flexibility he thought he could slide her under his legs along with his bound hands.

He stretched his arms out and brushed what he was pretty sure was her breast—much to the merriment of the audience. The next thing he knew, Lulu was up on tiptoe, walking over his head. The audience was going insane with cheers and laughter—until he ducked down and pulled back, sliding her legs along his chest until she lost her balance, landed in a straddle on his lap, with their tied hands high above them.

He felt every single centimeter of her body as if they were both completely naked. Her body heat met and married with his. Her breath fell in short, hot, puffs upon his mouth, just as he was sure his breath was landing on hers. Their eyes met and clashed. Both of them were frozen in one of those moments that communicated one solitary thing: desire.

She felt so good. Legs tucked round his hips… Her hips cinching with his… Breasts pushing into his chest, the taut tips of her nipples making it clear that she wanted him as much as he wanted her…

More than he ever had before, he wanted to throw away his dumbass rule book that made women off-limits. He wanted to forget about the *Will they? Won't they?* energy that had been running through him like adrenaline these past few weeks and open up his heart and his body to it all. He wanted to forget about the search and rescue games and spend the next three days in his room—or hers…it didn't matter. He wanted them to pour themselves into one another as if they were each molds that would make the other whole. He wanted to show her every level of pleasure he knew how to bring to a woman and explore all the others he had yet to learn.

Something about the way all the blood was rushing below his waistline told him that Lulu Kahale could wring him dry if she set her mind to it.

Somehow—miraculously—they both became aware of a countdown. Makoa and Kiko were still in deep discussion, their position unchanged. The audience was shouting a charged, "Five! Four! Three!"

"You okay with a bit of wrist burn?" Lulu asked, her lips brushing against his as she spoke.

It was the most erotic request for guaranteed pain that he'd ever received. "Yes."

She blinked, as if absorbing the deeper meaning of his assent—*I trust you*—then abruptly twisted her hands and yanked them free of the binding.

She leaped up in the air, hands held high, and danced around her brother and Kiko—who, seconds later, did a quick up-and-over arm-twist, as if they were performing a 1950s Lindy Hop, then faced one another, folded their hands together and slipped off the bands. Effectively achieving the required result without wanting to immediately have sex with one another.

The crowd went wild.

Zach rose and gave a red-faced bow, pleased for Lulu that they'd won, but hoping he could find the nearest exit—and fast. He didn't need congratulatory slaps on the back, or the celebratory mai tais already being called for at the Tiki Bar, or even the supersize T-shirt he and Lulu were meant to wear together, to prove they were the reigning champs of the team-building challenges. No. He needed a cold shower.

CHAPTER NINE

"You disappeared fast last night."

Lulu tried to make her tone and expression as neutral as possible. Zach was sitting at a table for one. If that didn't scream *Back the hell off*, she didn't know what did.

She nodded at his table when he took a sip of coffee instead of answering. "May I join you?"

"Please," he said, his tone much clearer than hers had been. It said, *Sure. You can sit down. But don't expect loads of chitchat.*

A shiver swept down her spine—and not because it was cold. This was the Zach Murphy she'd met on day one. The one who'd grounded her. The one who did everything by the book.

He was also the one she had thought was about as sizzling hot as a man could get, but was as much of an option for her on the dating front as a lemur.

Right then and there she realized she'd let all those barriers she'd kept up slide away. They'd kissed. She'd told him she thought about him naked. She'd climbed all over him as if he was her personal climbing wall and straddled him in front of the entire search and rescue corps.

And now it looked like he had made a decision. *Not today, buttercup. Not ever.*

Okay, then… If he wanted to be Mr. Rule Book again, she would focus on the fact that they were meant to be winning these games for the Oahu Search and Rescue crew today. She was a big enough girl that she could set aside the mountain of hurt that had weighted her chest when she'd seen him sneak out of the bar last night without so much as wishing her sweet dreams.

"You okay?" She pulled up a chair, plonked down her plate and took a bite of scalding-hot scrambled eggs, too proud to let him know they were burning the roof of her mouth. It helped relocate the pain in her heart, so…useful, really.

"Never better," he said.

"Liar," she countered.

He looked across and met her eyes.

His irises were the same color as the sea about a mile away from shore during a storm. Dark blue, fathomless and a bit overwhelming.

She swallowed. Had she messed up everything

last night by commandeering that final game instead of genuinely acting like a team member? *Screw it.* Teams needed leaders, and she'd led them to victory last night. She had even slept in that stupid T-shirt they'd awarded them, feeling the ache of loneliness at all the space in it that would've been filled by Zach if only she was normal and actually knew how to date someone.

They ate in silence for a few minutes, until she couldn't stand it anymore. They had the games to focus on, and if there was anything in the air between them that needed to be cleared they had about twenty-seven minutes to clear it before the first whistle blew.

"What's really going on?" she asked.

He shook his head. "Not important. Let's just focus on the games."

She bridled. "We *can't* focus on the games if you're going to be wandering around with a cloud over your head the entire time."

"I'm not—" He stopped himself and held up his hands, took a breath and regrouped. He looked her straight in the eye and, in the same guilty way he might've told her he had forgotten to fill out the Health and Safety forms for the weekend, said, "I wanted to have sex with you last night."

Lulu did a double take. She had, too. But she certainly wasn't going to confess as much to him. Unless… Would it make it easier if they both knew they wanted the same thing?

"Me, too."

He looked at her. Really looked at her. "We've been dancing round this like…like dancers," he finished lamely, tipping his head into his hands. He gave that gorgeous chestnut hair a scrub, then looked back up at her. "I can't think about anything else. It's driving me nuts."

"Me, too!" A smile bloomed on her face and her heart felt about a thousand times lighter. "I mean, this is totally not like me. I don't normally kiss the boss on training hikes."

Zach's lips twitched. "But you do mention thinking about them naked?"

"No." She swatted at the air between them and put on her *How very dare you?* face. "That's for special people," she said primly.

"Special people who also happen to be your boss and as a result are in a very difficult position?"

She tipped her head into her palm and made herself consider things from his angle. New job. New state. New life. Trying to set things up for his boy. Still on a probationary contract. A horny-as-hell colleague who kept pouncing on him.

No. It wasn't an ideal scenario.

Hardly believing she was proposing the idea, she tapped his plate with her fork to get his attention. "I could quit," she said.

"No." He instantly dismissed the idea. "No, you couldn't. I doubt you could even breathe without doing this job."

"Good point… But I like being a paramedic. I could do that full-time."

He laughed. "This isn't some weird team-building exercise, is it? Figuring out how we rearrange our lives so we can have sex?"

"No," she said, suddenly feeling the gravity of what they were really talking about.

Did they trust one another enough to be that close? Knowing there was a risk that it might all fall apart one day or…worse…that she might fall so head over heels in love that one day she'd have absolutely no control over the limits of how far she'd go to keep him safe?

She pressed her lips together, then released them. "I guess it's about deciding whether or not we want to change enough to break our own rules."

He sat back, threw his cloth napkin on top of his empty plate and considered her. "I know what some of your rules are and I seem to tick a lot of your don't-ever-go-there boxes."

"True."

"So..." He held his hands open. "If you haven't broken them for anyone else, why would you change them for me?"

Because she was pretty damn sure she was falling in love with him.

Instead, she said, "I'm beginning to wonder if all the rules and regulations I've imposed on my emotional life are holding me back professionally."

What a cop-out of an answer.

Unsurprisingly, he frowned. "What do you mean?"

She screwed her face up tight, then plumbed a level of honesty she rarely accessed. "I thought I wanted your job. Really, really wanted it. Not just so I could earn enough to buy my house. *Your* house," she swiftly corrected, making it clear it wasn't a dig, "And not just for the kudos. Or for proving to my brothers that I'm every bit as good as they are. Which, obviously, I am."

She gave a self-deprecating snort and then, seeing Zach's change of expression, made herself dial back the defensiveness.

Zach nodded for her to continue.

"The higher-ups even interviewed me for it, but they saw what I didn't."

"Which was…?"

"I would hate doing your job."

They laughed, and unnecessarily Zach asked, "Why?"

"It requires something I don't have." When he didn't say anything she filled him in. "*i* dotting… *t* crossing… I don't do those things."

Zach feigned being affronted, then the part of him that was unbelievably good at his job caught up with him and he conceded, "Your skills do lie outside the office."

No offense taken, she pushed on, feeling this conversation was one they shouldn't let go of. "Exactly. So I have to find a way to be content, knowing I'm not perfect."

His soft smile shifted into a frown. "No one's perfect."

He wasn't giving her an ego-boost. He was making a confession.

"There's a lot you don't talk about, isn't there?" she said carefully. "Some vein of hurt you don't ever want to tap into again?"

In that instant she saw that she'd hit on the truth. He had been hurt. Badly. Straight down to the marrow. And he never ever wanted to feel that type of pain again.

One of her grandmother's old Hawaiian sayings popped into her head. "Love is like a cleansing dew."

She had no idea if there was a future for her and Zach, but what she did know was that she cared enough for him and his son to throw herself in front of the proverbial bus for them. Which was both terrifying and exhilarating.

She put her hands on her pounding heart and said, "You can talk to me. What happens on the Big Island stays on the Big Island."

He huffed out a laugh. "I thought that was Vegas?"

She made a dismissive noise. "A girl can keep secrets wherever she pleases."

He shook his head and laughed, but then, to her surprise, he began to talk.

He talked about his ex-wife. How they'd met at a fire at a warehouse where some film crew had been doing a fashion shoot. She and a couple of the other models had been trapped. It had been scary. He'd had to carry her out over his shoulder and down a ladder to safety.

"Just like in the movies…" Lulu whispered, not exactly jealous of his ex, but wondering how on earth she could have ever walked away from someone who made her feel as safe as Zach could.

The relationship had grown from there. Zach and a couple of his colleagues had been asked to appear in a photo shoot. She'd asked him out. Actively pursued him from the sounds of things. So at least she had some brain cells.

Zach huffed out a laugh and brandished a ring-free hand. "But, as you can see, it didn't work out like in the movies. Not the kind with happy endings, anyway."

"What happened?" she asked.

"Harry happened," he said plainly.

Zach felt the shock of his blunt pronouncement as profoundly as Lulu seemed to. Her jaw literally dropped open and the hairs on her arms shot to attention.

Normally this would be the moment when the Lulu he'd come to know would hammer him with a thousand questions. She liked to know the details about everything.

It was something he hadn't originally noticed about her. His first impression had been that she was foolhardy. Reckless. But in actual fact, she calculated risk and response with lightning-fast accuracy.

He could see in her eyes that she felt the weight of what he was doing. Entrusting her with access to the darkest moments in his life.

A surge of empowerment replaced any anxiety he'd felt about laying himself bare to this woman. He wanted her to know the whole story. Know the whole man. If they were really going to explore this energy surging between them they both needed to know the truth. And the truth was he was a wounded warrior doing his damnedest to build a new life for his son.

So he continued to talk.

He told her that this was only the second time he'd put into words the real reason behind the failure of his marriage. That the first time had been when he and Christina had had that all-night, final, harrowing fight over who got to divorce who and why.

"If we hadn't had Harry, would we be having this conversation?"

In the end, he'd wished he hadn't asked. He'd already known the answer. Hearing it had felt like being filled with boiling oil. It had incinerated everything he'd believed to be true about love.

Even though they'd both known what had happened to Harry had been down to a mistake at the hospital—a cruel, critical loss of oxygen—she'd blamed Zach for Harry's disability. It was his job. His exposure to "unnatural elements." It had already crippled his father, she'd mocked. How long would it be before it did the same to him?

It was the same job that had brought them together, that had saved her life, and countless others during his career with the NYFD.

In that moment he'd seen their marriage for what it had always been. A photo opportunity. A photo opportunity that couldn't be sustained if their son was in the picture. And that simply hadn't been an option.

Lulu, despite the warm caramel color of her

skin and the heat of the early-morning sun, had turned ashen.

But, as if the story was a raging torrent long held back against the weakening walls of a dam that had finally burst, he kept on talking.

He'd never hated anyone or anything before. But he'd hated Christina at that moment. His entire world had turned black and white. There were two camps. Those who loved Harry and those who didn't. Which meant there were a lot of people in the wrong camp.

It had brought out a darkness in him that had both terrified him and fueled his rage. How could anyone reject their child? Let alone a gorgeous little boy who, through no fault of his own, faced more of life's hurdles than most?

He'd forced himself to imagine carrying that rage around with him for the rest of his life. Acknowledged how all-consuming it would be. How it would color absolutely everything. And as the words she was hurling at him had blurred into a high-pitched whisper-scream he'd had an epiphany.

Though every word she spat at him was laced with venom, she was whispering so as not to wake Harry. There *was* something in that seemingly arctic heart of hers. A tendril of affection for her son. He saw her anger for what it really was. Fear.

It had been a turning point for the pair of them.

Fear brought out the worst in some people, the best in others, and his wife had proactively walked across a line he knew he could never cross.

Lulu shook her head, as if absorbing it all was physically weighing her down. "What did you do?"

He'd taken a lot of long walks with Harry asleep in the stroller. Talked with his friends down at the station house. His parents. Harry's doctors. Strangers... It felt like he'd walked every inch of Manhattan and talked to every soul he'd met, trying to figure out what the hell to do.

"Hanging on to the rage wasn't an option. There was no way I could raise my son with my blood running cold every time I thought of Harry's mother. So..." His eyes caught on Lulu's mouth as her teeth pressed down on her lower lip, its deep red turning white from the pressure. He looked away and continued. "After some pretty deep soul-searching we opted to call a truce, cite irreconcilable differences as the reason for a divorce, and go our separate ways. Try to hang on to what good memories remained."

Lulu harrumphed in a way that suggested she would've found it every bit as tough as he had to find any good memories among the ashes of their short-lived marriage.

"Irreconcilable differences was a pretty apt way to describe it in the end. My ex didn't want to find out if she had the strength that parenting a disabled son would require, and I couldn't imagine not digging as deep as I could to do exactly that."

"But..." Lulu's voice cracked as she swiped at tears glossing her eyes. "Harry's great! I love that kid. I'd hang out with him every day of the week if I could."

Her voice was filled with fire, compassion and a need to defend a little boy who wasn't able to do it for himself. As if the little boy who had been rejected was her own.

Their eyes met and clashed, cinching in a shared disbelief that anyone could treat Harry in that way.

She'd never spoken so freely. So passionately. But now that she had he saw that it was true. She was always popping by for a quick surf lesson. Suggesting places to take Harry for burgers, shaved ice and who knew what else. Volunteering to cover for his parents if errands called.

Neither of them had put a name to what she'd become to them, their little tribe of two.

There was only one word for it.

Family.

But she had to know that his son was his priority. "Harry… Harry's the best thing that's ever happened to me," he said.

"And…" Lulu paused, visibly nervous about how to phrase her next question. "Does his mother see him at all? She must find it hard… You being so far away from New York."

The truth pressed against his chest and demanded oxygen. "She doesn't want to be a mom to a disabled kid. We've only been away for a few weeks, but from the day the divorce was finalized she's taken every overseas job offer going. Harry's not seen her for over a year."

Lulu looked as if this cruel slight to Harry had reached out and slapped her. "Gosh."

"Yeah," he agreed. "Gosh…" He traced his finger around a watermark on the table, then confessed, "It's probably been harder for me to wrap my head around than for Harry."

"How so?"

"She's never really been a hands-on mom. We had my parents' help at the beginning, of course. And specialists so we could understand just how much Harry's condition affected him. She would take him out on runs and things...you know, in his stroller. But as soon as she started working again, meeting up with her friends, I realized she only spent time with him when she absolutely had to."

Lulu whispered a heartfelt curse.

Zach nodded. "I know. I feel the same. But hanging on to that anger doesn't do Harry any good." He looked down at his hands, then back up into her eyes. "It's why seeing the friendship between the two of you develop has been so amazing."

He saw Lulu's gaze sharpen. They hadn't even defined whatever it was that was happening between the two of them, let alone what Lulu's relationship with his son was, but he knew she needed to know. "You're important to him. He talks about you all the time."

"He's a great kid."

Her voice was scratchy, and if he wasn't mistaken her eyes glossed over once again before she swept a palm across her face.

A whistle sounded and the emcee from last night's team-building games appeared at the edge of the dining room.

"Wheels up, everyone! Games commence in T minus ten!"

Lulu gave herself a wriggle, as if trying to clear herself of everything they'd just talked about, and when she looked at him there was something stronger, fiercer than in the looks they'd shared before.

"We're going to win these," she said, with a level of determination an army would've struggled to crush. "We're going to win these for Harry."

"Two more minutes!" Lulu insisted, one hand on top of the other, her body exhausted from the rhythmic compressions she'd been giving the "patient" they'd finally located far off the hiking trail.

It was well beyond the nine minutes of CPR most humans could receive without enduring severe and irreversible brain damage. Probably double that. Standard practice was to call time of death at twenty minutes, but there were some remarkable cases of thirty, forty and even fifty minutes of CPR preventing that crucial separation between life and death.

"Let me have a go." Zach held his hands over hers, ready to take over.

"No," Lulu growled, even while silently welcoming the heat of his hands above hers.

She wasn't cold—she was exhausted. But she couldn't stop. Not now. It was her fault it had taken them so long to find the CPR mannequin, cleverly kitted out with a device that allowed it to simulate having a heart attack. If she was successful a green light would ping on over its heart. If not the red light, already on, would turn black.

"Lulu…" Zach was using his *Be reasonable* voice. "If you exhaust yourself doing this, how are you going to have enough energy for the rope challenge?"

It was a good question.

Manhandling ropes in real life was tough.

Manhandling them in front of her giant of a brother after she'd drained all her strength on this exercise would be plain old humiliating. Especially when she'd have to throw them from one side of a ravine to another to "save" her partner.

Then she thought of Harry. Of how many hurdles he'd confronted during the course of his life. And another surge of strength replenished her waning stores.

Zach sat back on his heels, grim-faced, and watched her. He could've read her the riot act. Reminded her that this wasn't what the games were about. But something told her he knew why she was persisting. This mannequin represented a life. A real life they might very possibly have lost.

Two minutes later, the light on the mannequin's chest turned black.

The color seemed to fill her own chest with a cold, hollowed-out feeling that only equated with one thing: failure.

"Do you really think he's dead?" she asked, still giving syncopated compressions to the dummy's chest.

She was grateful for the rain, because she didn't want Zach to know she had begun to cry. She was furious with herself for having insisted they follow a line of broken palm fronds that any idiot could've seen were because of a fallen tree, not the trail of clues they were meant to have followed.

"I do," Zach said, pulling out a pocketknife. He stood up and started sawing a thick piece of bamboo.

"What are you doing?" she asked.

"Making a stretcher," he said, as if it was the most logical thing in the world.

Her respect for him doubled. They were going to carry back the "body." Offer it to its family along with the respect they deserved by giving them a chance to say goodbye to their loved one.

Despite the black light, she continued compressions as he worked, until eventually a small sob of despair escaped her throat and she fell back onto her heels, arms as limp as noodles, her energy stores utterly zapped.

"Hey!" Zach was by her side in an instant, pulling her into his arms, holding her so close she could feel his heart pounding against her palm. "You did everything you could."

"No!" she cried. "It wasn't enough."

She'd been wrong. This was her fault. Little Miss Mini-Menehune had insisted her knowledge of reading the jungle was better than Mr. Urban Jungle's.

Too tired to fight, she let Zach pull her closer, weeping into his saturated top. The rain was pummeling them as if its sole purpose was to remind them that they were mortals up against the might of Mother Nature and that sometimes—exactly like with her parents—all the search and rescue skills in the world would never be enough.

"Hey," he soothed. "It's only a game."

"It's not!" She pulled away from the warm comfort of his arms and began compressions again, ignoring the pain, ignoring the ridiculousness of it all. "It's so much more than that!"

"Tell me?"

Something about the openness with which he asked the question uncorked years of pent-up sorrow and frustration. Perhaps it was because Zach had pulled the Band-Aids off his own wounds this morning. Perhaps it was being on the Big Island, where her parents had first met. Perhaps it was falling in love with someone when she'd least expected it—two someones, father and son—and feeling as though she had absolutely no control over it.

And then, of course, there was the here and now. Not saving the life she'd been charged to save—the culmination of her biggest fears.

Her answers poured out of her in a torrent as she persisted with the compressions.

It was about her parents. About losing them so young. About spending a lifetime trying to prove to herself that if she'd been old enough she could've saved them. Could have swum harder, longer, stronger than anyone else, even though she knew it was both stupid and impossible, because sometimes "stupid and impossible" worked.

It was about her brothers. Trying to crawl out from underneath the endless safety precautions they'd put in place to look after her. Precautions she found suffocating rather than comforting. Stifling instead of enabling.

It was about having to fight and claw for every inch of progress she'd made in her career. And realizing, once she'd got there, that being at the top would never bring her parents back.

"Were their deaths preventable?" Zach asked, when she finally paused to take a breath.

"Yes!" Lulu wailed, unable to hold back the one thing she'd never been able to say out loud. "They could've stayed on the shore with *me*!" Her tears ran in hot, angry streaks down her cheeks and she didn't even care. "They could've chosen me and my brothers, but they didn't."

"What happened?"

In short, choky bursts she began, "My mom was working that day. As a lifeguard."

Zach nodded, readjusting his stance in a way that said he'd listen for as long as she needed him to.

"My dad had brought me down to the beach with a couple of my brothers to pick her up. An alarm went off—a surfer had gone out too far and was caught in the build-up of a storm. My—" The words snagged in her throat until she forced them out. "My mom went out to get him, even though they told her it wasn't safe. When she didn't come back, my dad told my brothers to look after me…he was going to get my mom. Neither of them ever came back."

The story sat between them as if it were an actual living thing. In a way, it was. Her parents' deaths lived in her every waking moment. Even in her dreams. The dreams where she got on her surfboard, beat the ocean at its own powerful game of chance and returned, triumphant, with both of her parents—only then she woke up in the darkness, still alone, still the choice her parents hadn't made.

It struck her that perhaps her own past was why she had taken to Harry so much. She hadn't been rejected by her parents in the way Harry's mother had walked away from him, but she certainly hadn't been their first choice. Her respect for Zach and his decision to take a job that was more desk-based than life-and-death-based went up about a thousand notches. He'd chosen his son over his job. Forever and always.

Zach was the first to break the silence. "You do know you're not to blame, right? That you're worth loving?"

She looked at him as if he was mad. "They chose death with each other over a safe life with us."

Zach shook his head as if he disagreed, but instead of saying as much he asked, "Why did you choose the same lifestyle? The same risks?"

"Isn't it obvious? I wasn't enough for them, so how on earth am I ever going to be enough for anyone else? I need to prove I can survive anything! Rescue whoever needs help, no matter what. I know it sounds insane, and that it'll never bring them back or change how people think about me, but I feel like I can't stop until I know *in here* that enough is enough."

She pressed her hand to her heart, feeling as

raw and as vulnerable as she ever had. What she was about to say could get her fired...

"I'm not there yet—I'm simply not there."

Zach didn't shake his head. Didn't laugh or mock. Instead, he got up and handed her his pocketknife. "I guess you'd better let me take over the compressions for a while. You finish the stretcher."

She did as he instructed, grateful for the activity. She'd exposed so many pent-up fears she was feeling overwhelmed by a sense of openness she hadn't felt before. Of possibility. There was a huge space inside her chest that she could choose to fill with hope or despair.

She looked at Zach, drenched to the bone, diligently giving compressions to a mannequin they both knew was "dead." He wasn't being insulting or derisive. Nor was he furious that they weren't going to win the games when he knew his boss had all but demanded a red-letter day.

He had held her. Comforted her. Refused to judge her. Even when she had literally led them down the wrong path and arrived too late to "save" their patient.

Her brothers would've berated her for not listening to them if, like Zach, they had suggested an alternative route and been shot down. But, rather than humiliate her, Zach's response to her mistake intimated that he knew the job wasn't black and white. It was about choices. Most of them good. Some of them bad.

And she was going to have to find a way to live with the bad ones—because while she'd never yet lost a patient in real life, it would happen. She could let it plunge her into a depression or she could take the ego-blow and learn the lesson. And in this case, the lesson was *Don't let your ego overpower your ability to work as a team.*

She'd grown too confident after this morning. The first contest had been a relatively easy rescue from a capsized boat about a kilometer offshore. While the other teams had wasted time flinging ropes and buoys and, courtesy of a choppy ocean, failing, she'd grabbed a buoy and dived into the sea, bringing the tie line directly to the capsized boat.

Much to her brother's annoyance, she and Zach had been able to shoot their flare two whole minutes before his team had.

But she'd made the decision to dive in on her own.

It should be a bitter pill to swallow. Realizing

how selfish she'd been. How myopic. Instead, Zach was giving her the space to learn that she could trust him. And with that came acceptance.

"Zach?"

He looked up, his shoulders steadily moving down and up, down and up, the fluid movements unrelenting even though they both knew it was pointless.

"I think we should call time of death."

"You sure?"

There wasn't a trace of scorn in his voice. He had her back. She felt the moment deeply, as if he had just offered her a part of himself in the same way she believed he'd offered himself to his son. Without reservation. With an abundance of love.

They called the time of death. Logged it into their phones. Loaded the "body" onto the stretcher.

She squatted down and stared at the manne-quin. "It's hard not to feel like a failure."

Zach's eyes shot to hers. "You are a lot of things, Lulu Kahale, but a failure is not one of them."

She wanted to believe him. She really did. And the fact that the words came from him meant the world to her. But it was as if he could sense that his words weren't quite penetrating deep enough.

He beckoned her to him. "C'mere, you."

She gratefully crossed to him, letting herself be fully absorbed into his comforting embrace. As he held her a soft glow of optimism warmed the open space in her chest. Trusting someone didn't have to be a place of fear. It could be a place of resilience. Possibility...

If she let it.

She looked up at him, wanting to put words to the gratitude she felt, but she couldn't.

He cupped her cheeks in his hands and dipped his mouth to hers. It was the softest kiss she'd ever known, instantly turning her insides liquid. Each kiss that followed felt potent with meaning, with strength. And with that strength she felt her resolve return. They had exposed their raw wounds to one another. Their biggest vulnerabilities. Their greatest fears. It added a new layer to their obvious attraction to one another. A depth to the supercharged lust that had been fueling their interactions.

Somehow they managed to pull apart from one another. "Should we get back to the base?" she asked.

From the heat in his eyes, she might as well have asked, *Your room or mine?*

They made quick work of hoisting up the stretcher, then followed the path they'd broken through the undergrowth. They made it back to the hiking trail with the mannequin strapped beneath a heat blanket, and just as the sun broke through the clouds they reached the finish line.

Her brother was there. Of course. And a handful of other teams.

"Hey, Mini!" her brother shouted, throwing her a bottle of water. "We were about to send out the search parties."

"Ha-ha," she deadpanned.

He looked at her. Really looked at her. He dropped the attitude. "You okay?"

For the first time she felt as if he was going to listen to her answer and take it at face value. "Yeah," she said, throwing a smile at Zach. "I'm good."

Mak glanced at the body on the stretcher, then asked, "How long did you guys attempt resuscitation?"

"Over an hour."

He made a whooping noise and whistled. "Mini? You are a legend."

She and Zach threw one another questioning glances. "Why? We didn't resuscitate him."

"Maybe not, but you've always believed in trying your hardest. Respect." He held up a fist for her to bump. He looked over his shoulder at the pack of competitors, each throwing back deep slugs of water or kneading sore muscles. "None of us did over twenty minutes."

She and Zach shared another smile, this one shot through with a fresh, energizing sense of achievement—and then, because it was Zach, the look intensified into something far more intimate.

Mak didn't miss the exchange.

She braced herself, prepared for him to thwack one of his tree trunk arms over Zach's shoulders and take him on a little walk and talk to explain how things worked in the Kahale family.

Instead, he gave her a light punch on the arm and said, "I'm guessing you two probably need a long hot shower before the luau?"

Lulu practically choked on her surprise. Was her brother telling her he *approved*?

Mak gave a double *shaka* sign and congratulated them on a job well done, then left the pair of them standing there, temporarily speechless.

The only thing remaining between them now was a question she was too nervous to ask.

Do you want me?

Zach broke the silence first.

"I'm guessing this isn't the best way to show up to a luau." He looked down at his filthy outdoor gear, caked in red, iron-rich island mud.

Lulu instantly pictured herself peeling that top off him and scrubbing him clean. Heat darted into areas of her body she hadn't realized could light up with lust.

Shakily, she said, "The luau's not for a couple of hours."

"Maybe you could help me pick out the best shirt to wear?"

Lulu's eyes shot to Zach's. "I—I could do that. If you trust me."

Zach's eyes dropped to her mouth as she spoke. It felt tactile, his gaze...

She swallowed and reflexively licked her lips. "I trust *you.*"

Those three words... He knew how much they meant to her.

She became aware of her breasts growing heavy—not under the weight of the wet, muddy top, but under the weight of his eyes, which were noticing—yup—her nipples standing to attention.

"I should probably change, too," she managed.

"Mmm… And I'd better call Harry. A quick check-in."

"Yeah." She felt herself brighten. "Harry would be proud of you."

"Of us," Zach corrected.

And just like that they became an "us." She'd never been an "us" before. Sure, she'd dated. Had boyfriends. But none she'd ever really admitted to. It was like trying on a dress she'd never thought she'd look good in and realizing it made her look absolutely beautiful.

Us.

The word was catapulted to the top of her list of Most Wonderful Words in the World.

Us.

It even tasted good.

Zach shifted his weight, his eyes pinging to the hotel and back. He was making a decision. A big one. A single dad with a disabled kid wasn't going to let just anyone into his heart space, let alone his bed.

She held her breath.

His eyes met hers, decision made. "Apparently there's a really good club sandwich on the room service menu. I know the luau's coming up, but I'm a bit hungry now. We could call Harry... Go over tomorrow's schedule... Line our stomachs a bit before we try another one of those mai tais."

We.

Us.

"Good idea," Lulu said. Or maybe she didn't.

They were so busy staring at one another, trying to figure out what this new world order was, she didn't really have a clue what was happening.

Maybe they'd stand here all day, staring at one another like lovestruck idiots.

Maybe her brother would find them at midnight and clonk their heads together and point out the obvious. They needed to get a room.

Maybe they'd be struck by lightning.

Eventually—mercifully—one or both of them started walking. The outdoors became the indoors. One corridor led to another, and then the elevator, and then another corridor, and then, without so much as a word passing between them, they found themselves outside Zach's hotel room.

He tugged the key out of his back pocket. "You good with this?"

She nodded. She was. And there wouldn't be any need for the room service menu. She had everything she needed right in front of her.

CHAPTER TEN

THE SECOND THE door clicked shut Zach felt every chain he'd wrapped around his heart unlock and drop to the ground. He felt free in a way he hadn't in years.

At last. The fight was over. Resisting his attraction to Lulu hadn't made him stronger, wiser, or better able to defend his son. It had hobbled him. And Harry. And Lulu. And holding either of them back was the last thing he wanted to do.

He looked at her as if seeing her entirely anew.

Smart, funny, feisty, fiery, sexy Lulu. The ying to his yang. The fire to his ice. All of the opposites combining into something better, not worse.

Today his attraction to her had deepened into something he'd thought he'd never feel again. Love. Or at least the beginnings of it. He trusted her. With his heart and his son's. It was a powerful realization.

She looked up at him, those amber eyes of hers glinting through the inky darkness of her lashes. There was an openness in her expression he hadn't seen before. It wasn't vulnerability. It was consent. Belief. And unfettered desire.

"Should we call Harry?"

"Definitely."

He put his phone on speaker, and when Harry answered they described the day to him, their eyes glued to one another as they spoke, peeling off their boots and shoes. When the call ended they were still staring at one another, their breath coming short and fast as if they'd just run up a mountain. And in a way, they had. Both of them had opened up, baring their most vulnerable selves to the other, and had emerged from their admissions not only unscathed, but cared for. Deeply so.

His erection came so hard and fast he heard the leather on his belt strain in protest. He'd never wanted anyone more than he wanted Lulu, and from the dark gold glimmer of her eyes she felt the same way.

"You're shivering," he said.

"It's cold," she said.

It wasn't. She was shaking with adrenaline. So was he.

"Before we do anything..." He stopped and

cleared his throat. "Um… Do we need to define what this is?"

"It's us," she said. "Trying to figure out what this is."

He nodded. Yeah. That was good. But… "Not much of a courtship…us hating each other at first sight."

"It wasn't hate," she countered. "It was…frustration."

He quirked his head to the side and nodded. That was right, too. "We're very different."

"That's not always a bad thing."

"What if it becomes a bad thing?"

"What if it doesn't?"

He smiled.

She smiled back.

So it was settled. They were going to see what this was. No matter the outcome.

"Shower?" she asked, her eyes doing a quick scan of their muddy and rain-drenched clothes.

He took her hand in his and, without bothering to take her clothes off, led them straight under the rainforest shower heads in the huge wet room.

He'd been upgraded by the hotel, but hadn't thought a thing of it until now. The wet room was otherworldly, bringing the outdoors inside. It had two walls of bamboo, and the water was dewing on the surface, creating a tiny waterfall on the beautifully tiled shower bench. The other two "walls" were retractable glass doors that led onto a small, private rooftop garden, filled with lush tropical plants.

He threw them open, relishing everything he'd barely noticed the night before. With Lulu by his side the setting was pretty damn sexy. Then again, he would've happily made love to her just about anywhere right now. They could've been in a double wide trailer or a palm leaf shack for all he cared. But adding the element of luxury to this long-awaited moment was a very nice cherry on top of a long-awaited sundae.

He tipped her chin up and dipped his mouth to hers, then kissed her hard, enjoying the way her lips felt like that first incredible sensation of biting into a soft-serve ice cream cone. Yielding, but rewarding. Mouthwatering in a way that only made him want more.

Though they had both literally dragged themselves through the jungle, she somehow managed to taste of vanilla, mint and coconut. He didn't think he'd ever tire of the taste of her. And this was just the tip of the iceberg. Kissing. Standing in a shower with nothing more than a couple of flimsy T-shirts between them.

An insatiable hunger built inside him. It was beyond anything he'd felt before.

He'd thought what he and his ex had shared ranked up there, but he'd not had a clue.

His body's response to Lulu was in another league.

Holding her in his arms, tasting her, touching her…her back, her waist, her hips…he felt as if he was being consumed whole by an unquenchable thirst.

Knowing that he could trust her, that she cared for him and his son—loved his son, even, and possibly loved him—meant more than he could ever put words to. He and Harry came as a unit, and until this moment he'd never realized how braced he'd been, ready to be found wanting because of it.

To Lulu, it seemed it was an asset. Having a boy so filled with love. Joy. Just like she was.

His kisses deepened. He wanted her. All of her. Taste. Touch. Sound. Pleasure. Pain. *All of it.*

"Wow…" she whispered against his lips as he turned on the matching shower heads.

"It's no Turtle Hideaway, but…"

"It'll do."

Lulu play-growled, grabbing fistfuls of his T-shirt and tugging him closer to her. Their lips met again, and his body felt saturated by an all-consuming temperature explosion. Lava meeting lava. Impact succumbing to immersion. It was impossible to know where he began and she ended. He didn't want to know. All he wanted was Lulu. Everything that made him who he was—common sense, lists, rules—was being swept into the drain along with the water pouring round the pair of them, energizing them as if it were a life-affirming ambrosia.

He felt her hands unceremoniously ruck up his T-shirt, her fingers pressing against his skin, tracing the lines of his stomach muscles, inching their way ever upwards, as if trying to commit the terrain of his torso to memory. Until, impatiently, she pushed his T-shirt up and over his head, her mouth leaving his only to find purchase on his nipples. Her tongue gave each one hot wet swirls of approbation, and her groans of pleasure at the sensation of skin on skin vibrated through to his chest. His heart. He'd never imagined being on fire would feel this good.

He slipped his fingers under her top and slowly…achingly slowly…pulled it up, enjoying feeling her body quiver in response to his touch.

"Take it off," she begged. "I want to feel you against me."

She was doing that, all right. Her hips were pressed into that sweet space that seemed to have been molded just for her, where his erection was taking on a life of its own…pulsing, demanding attention. If she so much as touched it with the tip of one of her fingers…

He grabbed her wrist as she began tugging at the clasp on his belt. "No."

"Yes."

Her chest arched into his, her hips nestling in closer, daring him to deny her access to all that strained at the fabric of his trousers. *Hell.* Every single pore in his body was aching to burst out of his clothes, rip hers off and take her right here and now on the tiled floor, but…

"Not yet."

"I want you naked. Now." Her voice was throaty. Hungry.

"When I say so."

Something flickered in her eyes. On and off. On and off. She was rewiring her response to him. Twenty-four hours ago Lulu would've let him have hell for being so absolute.

Half-naked, ravenous, horny, today's Lulu kind of liked it…handing the reins of control over to him. Her fingertips pressed into him as if she was trying to divine which direction to go. Push or pull. Take or be taken.

He saw the lights flick on again—full beam. She went up on tiptoe, leaning into him but not against him. "All right, then, Mr. Boss Man," she whispered into his ear, nipping his lobe as she paused for breath. "Have it your way."

He took the reins she'd just handed him and held on tight.

Her hunger for him made prolonging the moments of discovery all the more pleasurable. Finding the beauty mark just to the left of her belly button… The tiny tattoo of a starfish hidden between her ring and index fingers… The small scar etched into the divot between her hip and her rib cage…

"Coral…" she breathed against his neck as he traced his finger along the bump.

He didn't know how he did it, but he took his time.

Eventually, when she threatened to rip her own

clothes off, and his too while she was at it, he pulled her T-shirt up and over her head. Her hair fell free of the messy topknot she'd stacked it in, a slick of ebony cascading down her back.

He ran his hands over and through it as if it was one of the seven wonders of the world. "Let me wash it."

She looked up at him, surprised. "No one's asked to do that before."

"Well, I'm asking now."

"Why?"

There was the smallest hint of fragility in her voice. Defensiveness.

"I'd like to do it. Consider it my gift to you before I ravage you."

She pulled him to her again, and he felt the small triangles of her lace bra rub against his chest, the tight nubs of her nipples straining against the fabric.

"I want you," she whispered.

He wanted her, too. But he was enjoying this. Not just touching and holding her. It was the trust she was giving him. The openness. He wanted her to enjoy the luxury of caring and being cared for.

Lulu had locked the door of her emotional cupboard long ago. Way back when her parents had died, actively refusing help from anyone from that point forward.

He took the shampoo bottle off the small teak shelf, but she steered his hand back and he put it down.

"Why don't you want me to wash your hair?" he asked.

She hesitated, then said, "Because I won't be able to see your face."

He got it. They were both on new terrain.

He put her hand on his belt buckle. "Go on. Take it off."

He was handing back the reins. Letting her know this could go at whatever pace she wanted, stop or start whenever she blew the whistle—because this was something they had to do together, or they weren't going to do it at all.

Her fingers trembled for a moment. She looked up at him and then, decision made, took that belt buckle and whipped it out of its belt loops so fast he heard the clatter of the buckle on the tiled floor before he felt the exquisite release of his erection from his trousers.

He stepped out of the pile of saturated cotton and used his foot to flick it away. Lulu was right.

Even a solitary thread of fabric between them was too much.

"Oh, my goodness me," she said, in a voice double-dipped with approval.

Her tongue swept across her lips. An intense pulse of longing throbbed deep inside him.

"May I return the pleasure?" he asked, his fingers hitching onto the waistline of her hiking trousers.

"Please..." she managed, her eyes still glued to his arousal.

He dropped to his hands and knees, hushing her protests that his moving wasn't fair because his body was too far away now as he undid the waist tie of her trousers and tugged them down in a oner. He threw them on top of his.

"Now," he said, sitting back on his heels and sliding his hands along her legs up to the perfect curve of her butt. "Now it's fair."

As he rose she pushed him back, so that he was forced to sit down on the bench. The energy between them flashed and morphed into yet another form. Neither of them was in charge now. It was as if they'd handed this moment over to the more primitive parts of their hearts—their souls—leaving their bodies to respond organically to each other.

He pulled her to him so that she was straddling him, his arousal taut and pressing against her belly. He undid the front clasp of her bra, felt his breath catching in his throat at her sheer beauty. A completely naked Lulu...right here on his lap. She was so perfect he could hardly breathe.

If he were to have conjured up his own Aphrodite to step out of a seashell and into his arms it would have been Lulu. He lightly stroked each of her breasts, cupping them, tracing them, and when her nails clawed into his back, her hips ground into his, he pulled one of her nipples into his mouth as he rubbed the pad of his thumb against the other nipple, enjoying her whimper of response.

"We need protection," she eventually managed. "Now."

He thanked just about every god there was that his friends back at the firehouse in New York had stuffed his toiletries bag with condoms on his last day. At the time he'd been certain they'd never be used. Now he wondered if there would be enough. He and Lulu were here on the Big Island for two more days, and from the way his body responded to hers they'd be needing that do-not-disturb sign for quite some time.

They turned off the shower and threw towels at one another, not caring if they were fully dried or not. He charged her with putting the sign on the door while he unearthed a fistful of condoms. When she got to the bed, a big huge fluffy towel wrapped round that gorgeous, curvy body of hers, he held them up.

She arced an eyebrow. "Hmm…" she said, her smile turning decidedly wicked. "Seems like we've got a busy night ahead of ourselves."

Lulu had engaged in foreplay before. But never like this.

Being with Zach Murphy was like taking a master class in the senses. Learning one by one which of the pleasure zones did what and why. To the point where she almost felt guilty.

Almost.

Every second they'd spent together in the shower had shifted her low-grade hum of desire into a pounding, pulsing, energized ache. She wanted to throw herself into his arms. Impale herself on him. Tempt him. Torture him. Torture herself.

He tugged her to him, teasing away the tuck of the towel between her breasts as if he had all the time in the world. Every brush of his fingertips on her skin made her feel something new. Shimmery. Hedonistic. Carnal.

And above all completely safe.

She didn't have an ounce of fear that Zach Murphy would ever hurt her. Emotionally or physically. He had been so open with her about his past, so generous when she'd dumped a thousand pounds of pent-up misery on him earlier today, she was literally in awe of the generosity of his lovemaking.

He let the towel slip down along her body, the thick cotton skidding along her curves as if it had been specially designed to add another level of eroticism to the moment. She felt sexy and strong in a way she never really had before. Proud to stand in front of him without a stitch of clothing on, letting him drink her in as if he'd just crawled across a desert and she was a tall, cool glass of water he wanted to savor and gulp down.

Normally she would've been diving under the covers at this point, demanding the lights be turned off and all eyes shut as "the games" began.

But this was no game.

This was real life.

Someone like Zach—a man who'd loved and lost and been bruised like hell in the process—wouldn't be looking for a fling. He was an all-or-nothing kind of guy and this, right here and now, was his way of saying he was in.

He'd made it very clear she had a choice in the matter, too.

All.

Or nothing.

How could she not choose all? She was in love with him. Felt safe with him. Felt secure in a way she'd never felt with another man. She adored his son. Couldn't imagine a world without either of them.

She felt as if she'd lived a lifetime in these past eight hours, never mind the previous few weeks. She'd treated him like the enemy, had behaved like an idiot, then fallen in love with his son, with him, told him her secrets, fallen apart, pulled herself back together again and still he was here. Wanting her. Hungry for her.

It struck her that she'd been so busy holding that steel trap around her heart with one hand and a spear in the other, ensuring whoever she was with knew that she called the shots—*all* of them—she'd never fully opened herself up to the possibility that a relationship didn't have to be like that. Combative. Competitive.

It could be *this*. A shared energy that only made her want to be a better person. Everything about Zach filled her with peace. Well, sexy lust, too, but there wasn't anything about him that was in competition with her. He exuded an energy that made it very clear he didn't need to show her how male he was. How powerful. Zach Murphy wasn't proving anything to anyone. The only thing he was doing was making it very clear that he wanted her. And that made him the most alpha male she had ever met in her life.

He could have her with or without a pretty bow on top. In fact, it was time he learned how great it felt to have the spotlight thrown on him.

She pushed him onto the bed. Her hand barely met with resistance as she put it on his sternum and guided him back to the huge nest of pillows before climbing on top of his lap and straddling him. She felt protected and wild. Drunk on hormones and yet more sane than she'd ever felt before. She felt honest and true. But most of all she felt as if a passion bomb had exploded in her.

She was hot and wet and physically aching to feel him inside her.

After eliciting a few short, sharp breaths from him while she unfurled the condom on his beautiful erection, she lifted herself up a bit, using his shoulders as ballast, and then slowly, achingly slowly, she began to lower herself onto him.

Once she felt him fully inside her she began to rock her hips, amazed that she had been able to take all of him into her. His movements began to match hers. Soon they were moving with a synchronicity she wouldn't have believed possible. Action overwhelmed her ability to think straight. She tried to memorize every movement, savor each touch, each kiss, but the surges of pleasure completely washed away her ability to form a coherent thought.

They clutched at one another. Gave featherlight kisses. Tickled. Ravaged. Gasped. Groaned. Everything the senses allowed, she felt. And when, after she didn't know how many minutes or hours, they reached a mutual climax, they clung to one another as if their lives depended upon it. Shuddering and shaking in each other's arms as if they'd been taken apart and rebuilt again.

And in a way she had. She had never been more honest in her life than she had just been with Zach. She'd given herself to him completely. If she could unzip him and crawl inside him, give him everything he needed—extra heart-beats, more energy, more stamina, iron, magnesium, whatever it was he needed—she'd give it to him.

She slid off his big man chest onto the mattress. He rolled on his side and curved himself around her. His warm, muscled belly against her back… His thigh hair tickly against her bare legs… His breath on her neck, softer and sweeter than a breeze off the ocean… They dozed and nestled, all thoughts of attending the luau as far away as the moon.

When she woke, his arms were wrapped around her as easily as if he'd been doing it for years and the room was dark. She could smell him on her skin and herself on his. It made her hungry for more. She snuggled against him and, feeling his arousal against her bottom, was instantly ravenous for more.

Something told her it was going to be a long night—but the kind of long night she would happily stay up for.

CHAPTER ELEVEN

ZACH PULLED LULU'S wetsuit off the outdoor shower towel rail and hung it behind the curtain, out of sight. He smiled as yet another round of raucous laughter sounded from the beach, where Lulu and Harry were building sand castles.

She was a proper engineer when it came to bucket and spade architecture, drilling into Harry how critical it was to build the moat first, so that when the tide inevitably came in to try to sweep away their craftsmanship it stood a bit more of a chance against the inevitable.

The thought snagged and jarred as he caught himself pulling her bikini off the outdoor line and stuffing it into the laundry basket he had on his hip. It was almost exclusively filled with Lulu's belongings.

Zach was hosting a staff barbecue at his place this afternoon, which meant tidying up was inevitable. But why was he only picking up Lulu's things, with a plan to stow the basket out of sight under the bed?

Okay, sure… It had been three weeks since they'd returned from the games, and they'd stuck to their agreement to keep their relationship private. Zach was still on probation, and they were both pretty sure that the—*ahem*—new level of relations between the pair of them would be frowned upon, but…

What exactly were they doing, here? Were they keeping their relationship private for professional reasons, or was it because both of them had concerns? Big ones.

From the outside, it looked a picture-perfect blossoming romance.

They spent a lot of time together. Pretty much all their time outside of work. And most of it here at Turtle Hideaway. No holding hands and gazing into one another's eyes over a candlelit table in the center of Honolulu for the two of them.

Was this secluded cove their moat against the rest of the world? A place to soak up as much of this loved-up feeling as they could before the inevitable occurred and the bubble popped?

He could almost see it playing out before him. The moment when their ying and yang views of the world were no longer the perfect combination but diametric opposites.

He hadn't missed the fact that they were still clashing at work, with Lulu pushing for the team to respond faster, harder, not taking the time to weigh up health and safety, until Zach stepped in and demanded it. He'd written off her behavior as a bit of a show for the rest of the team. But did it run deeper than that? Perhaps Lulu simply couldn't break free of that built-in need to press her full weight against any sort of restraint...

He shook his head. He didn't know. He just didn't know. And he had a little boy's heart to look after.

A collective cry of dismay came up from the beach, along with a wash of waves.

He heard Lulu's, "High five, li'l buddy," and, "Good work."

Ten minutes ago that would've been enough to assure him he was right to trust her with his son's heart. But now, as if letting one single solitary doubt through a razor-thin gap in their little love bubble, the floodgates opened.

He looked at the basket again. Keeping his job was important. Keeping Lulu felt just as important. But was respecting him and what he'd been through as important to her?

Harry and Lulu appeared from the beach. Her arm was wrapped around his shoulder and the two of them were oohing and ahhing over a shell one of them had found.

Guiltily, Zach stowed the laundry basket in the outdoor shower stall, out of sight. His son was his priority. So, for now their relationship was going to have to stay under wraps.

"Nice to have a break from the rains, isn't it?" Casey asked.

"Mmm..."

Lulu was half listening to Casey and half enjoying the sight of Zach manning the barbecue. He was wearing an apron. Board shorts, a T-shirt and some flip-flops completed his ensemble. Now that his tan had deepened and his body language had shifted from East Coast uptight to Hawaii's much more relaxed Island Time, he almost looked as if he was going to live here forever.

As if sensing her gaze on him, he turned and looked at her. A little zap of excitement spiked her pulse as their eyes met. And then a sliver of concern. Ever since she and Harry had come back from the beach this morning he'd been a bit off.

Maybe this whole inviting the team to his house thing wasn't really his jam. Or, more worryingly, maybe she wasn't.

"Want your burger medium rare or medium?" he called.

"Medium, please," Lulu yelled across the small group.

He gave her the guy chin-tilt thing, then turned back to the grill.

Hmm… Something was up with him. Definitely.

"Someone's happy with her New York beefcake." Casey elbowed her in the ribs, her eyes flicking between her and Zach.

Lulu feigned a shocked expression. "The boss man, you mean? *Pfffft*."

Casey snorted, then turned her voice singsong. "Lulu's got a boyfriend."

"Shut up!"

Casey grinned, but then her expression sobered. "I'm totally happy for you two, but remember…he actually *is* the boss. And he's got a kid. And…baggage."

Lulu bristled. "We've all got baggage."

"I know. Cool your jets. I'm just saying…letting down a guy like that and a kid like that when you get tired of playing house… It'll be tough."

Every nerve ending in Lulu's body shot to high alert. Had Casey tapped into Zach's weird energy? Or had he…? No. He wouldn't have confided in Casey. Would he?

"I'm not playing house," she replied hotly.

Casey cackled and gave her the side-eye. "How long have you wanted to live in this house?"

Lulu's nose hitched up. Years. And Casey knew that. The question was clearly rhetorical. She didn't answer.

"And how about this new thing of volunteering at the Superstars Surf Club?"

"I've been doing that for ages."

Casey's eyebrows shot up. "Regularly?"

Okay. Maybe not regularly. But enough to have the place mean something to her. A lot, actually. And definitely enough for Casey's line of conversation to throw her hackles up.

"I hope you're not suggesting I orchestrated this whole thing." She was a lot of things, but conniving was not one of them.

"No, not at all," Casey said. "Seriously. Not at all. It's just...you seem to be moving pretty fast."

"I told you. We're not a couple."

"Then why is there a laundry basket in the outdoor shower full of your stuff?"

Zach had hidden her things away? Her tone turned icy. "Harry and I do a lot of swimming here."

"In your pajamas?"

Lulu stood up, properly angry now. What was this? The Spanish Inquisition?

Casey made a soothing gesture. "I'm just saying—this is the most serious I've ever seen you about someone and I'm trying to figure out when to prepare myself for the fallout."

What the hell...?

"What are you suggesting, Casey? That I set this whole thing up so I could dump him? Make bunny stew?"

"No, not at all." Casey gave an easy laugh. "Chill. Seriously. I'm not saying you did any of this on purpose, it's just..."

"It's just what?" Lulu demanded.

Casey lowered her voice and put her entire focus on Lulu. "He's got a lot of things you've wanted for a long time, but maybe it'd be smart to prepare him for the fallout when…you know… you decide to move on."

Shards of understanding lanced straight through her heart as she suddenly saw what Casey saw.

Her house.

Her job.

A beautiful little boy who loved learning how to surf.

A ready-made family tailored just for her.

Walking away from perfection would be insanity.

She wouldn't do that to Zach and Harry.

Would she?

"I'm thirsty," Casey announced, as if the topic was over. "Want a lemonade?"

Lulu nodded. Anything to get Casey away from her before she began stuffing everything she'd said back down her throat.

Casey's angle on the situation was off. Lulu wasn't living on fantasy island. Everything that was happening was real. *Very* real. Genuine. How dare she suggest Lulu would cut and run?

She pulled herself up short. Casey had known her a long time. They weren't the talk-on-the-phone-for-hours kind of friends, but they knew each other well. Casey knew her weak spots. Her tendencies. And Lulu's track record was almost exclusively devoted to diving in, surfacing, then walking away before so much as a bruise could appear on her heart.

She sat on top of the picnic table she and Casey had been leaning against and tried to squash all the questions Casey's interrogation had un-leashed. She took deep breaths. Counted waves. Tried to let the happy-go-lucky energy of the small gathering surround her again.

Nope. No good.

She was properly agitated.

Ten minutes ago she wouldn't have believed feeling as happy and relaxed as she had was pos-sible.

But the happiness obviously had fault lines. Casey had managed to crack the veneer of it with barely so much as a tap.

It was horrifying revelation when, just this morning, lying in Zach's arms, she'd thought being with him "stilled her," as her grandmother would say. Not when they were naked, obviously. But there was something about opening her heart up to him that made her feel stronger than she ever had. And giddier. She was falling head over heels in love with a strait-laced guy from New York City.

Maybe that was exactly the problem.

Opposites might attract, but how often did their relationships succeed? Maybe Zach was the one who was planning on doing the dumping, but had yet to figure out how to tactfully extract her from his and Harry's lives? Maybe she was just a rebound fling?

He wouldn't make her stop being friends with Harry, would he?

Now that the hounds of doubt were prowling round her brain, she thought maybe it was a good thing she'd not told him she loved him.

Or maybe it was old Lulu, justifying not committing again.

She sat there, shell-shocked, as if Casey's pronouncements and Zach's weird mood were physically chipping away at her confidence.

"Lulu!"

Her frown turned into a smile as Harry ran toward her, up on tiptoes, arms windmilling with excitement as they so often did, with the big starfish of sunblock she'd painted on his face when he'd complained a single stripe wasn't any fun.

"Look!" He held out a seashell as if it were a precious jewel.

She cooed over it and held it up, appreciating the gorgeous pearlescent colors.

He looked wistfully out at the sea, then back at her. "Are we going surfing tomorrow?"

She gave him a double thumbs-up and made a Herculean effort to attach a smile to it, because everything she'd thought she was sure of ten minutes ago was now being obliterated in a huge bubbling pot of insecurity stew.

"Absolutely," she made herself say. "Wild horses couldn't keep me away."

And they wouldn't.

It was one thing if Zach wanted to call their relationship quits, but there was no way she was letting Harry down the way his mother had. None.

"When do you think I'll be able to surf like you?" Harry asked.

Her heart twisted into a knot. She ruffled his hair and said, "It took me years, little man."

It wasn't a lie. But it wasn't the full truth. He'd never be as good as she was because of his disability. But why strip him of the joy of trying?

A huge, overwhelming urge to burst into tears

consumed her. Over the past few weeks it had been watching interchanges like this pass between father and son that had made her fall even more in love with Zach than she already was.

His quiet, disciplined inner strength was one of the simplest and most beautiful joys to behold. He knew better than anyone that his son had limits, but he did his best to let him explore the outer reaches of those limits. It was a level of parenting bravery that there should be medals for. Heck—her brothers struggled with the fact that she did search and rescue to this day, despite her being at the top of her class in just about everything apart from size. She couldn't imagine what it was like for Zach. Especially knowing Harry's mother had lacked the strength to love her son as much as Zach did. Had rejected him even—rejected both of them. It genuinely did not compute.

She pulled Harry in for a hug, loving the openness with which he wrapped his arms round her waist, gave her a huge squeeze and then, with the same happy, wild energy, ran over to his father to do the same to him.

Her joy felt bittersweet when Zach gave a big "Oof..." as Harry careered into him, deftly shifting them both away from the grill with a gentle, "Easy there, H-man. Eyes on the prize."

She loved how Zach's body language changed when he was with his son. The way he handed him the tongs to take over hot dog–turning duties, his arm sliding over his son's slim shoulders. Protective, but not restrictive. She loved the way he called him "H-man" or "son" with the same level of pride an athlete might say they'd won a gold medal or a scientist a Nobel Prize. He thought his son was a wonder and his pride showed.

He was the gentlest, most patient, greatest dad she'd ever met. And that was saying something. Because, even though they annoyed the living daylights out of her, her brothers already had pole positions in that department. Seeing them with their little kids… It was something else.

Her smile faded a bit as her brothers crept into her consciousness. Would they be thinking the same things Casey was? That she lacked commitment and would leave Zach before he had a chance to leave her?

She shot a glare in Casey's direction, grateful that she'd been sidetracked by Stewart's retelling of a recent sea rescue the pair of them had pulled off.

What did she know?

Lulu had introduced Zach to both Makoa and her grandmother. Which was huge. No one she'd ever dated had met her grandmother. Sure, they'd accidentally run into her at a shaved ice stand, but she hadn't cut and run, or turned Zach and Harry around and walked the other way. She'd introduced them like the adult woman she was, only leaving out the part about how she was falling head over heels in love with the pair of them.

All of which meant... Casey might be right.

The table she was sitting on abruptly shifted, lurching her sideways, as if her brother had come and sat on the other side to send her off balance. She whirled round to tell him off, but no one was there.

Her eyes shot to Zach, who was catching some hot dogs that were falling off the grill while holding up Harry with his other hand.

All the conversations that had been light and cheery turned into a swift volley of, "Did you feel that?" Followed up by, "Was that an earthquake?"

There were thousands of earthquakes a year in

Hawaii, most of them low grade, but all worth paying attention to. This one hadn't felt big enough to trigger a tsunami, but it was always important to check.

All the locals began kicking into action. Getting Zach to put out the barbecue. Checking their phones for tsunami warnings. Discussing their designated safe spots at a higher elevation. Figuring out who had brought their first aid run kits in their cars.

For the first time ever, Lulu felt completely paralyzed. Normally she would've been the first to leap into action, helping the most obvious candidate who needed it, who in this case was Harry. If there were aftershocks, he'd need someone to help talk him through it all. She'd be organizing people into cars. Checking her own phone.

But she couldn't move.

Casey's words were pounding against her brain like dead weights.

Letting down a guy like that and a kid like that when you get tired of playing house... It'll be tough.

Lulu's phone began vibrating. Then she heard Zach's ring. And Casey's. Phones rang one after the other—until she realized what they'd felt was an aftershock. Something big had already happened.

She wouldn't have a chance to clear out her brain or to talk her worries out with Zach. They were all going to work. And whatever it was that awaited them was going to push them all to the limit.

Zach listened intently to the voice on the end of the phone. His eyes snapped to Lulu's as the information he was receiving sank in.

One of her brothers was missing in a landslide. Duke. The stuntman. A movie company had been filming a chase scene on quad bikes for the blockbuster they were shooting. Duke and a stuntwoman had been riding up along some of the island's steepest ridges and the clifftop they'd been riding on had given way. It wasn't looking good.

Lulu was also on the phone, presumably hearing the same news. She was staring at him. Hard.

It was a strange look. One he couldn't read. He wanted to kick himself for being cool with her all afternoon. If he'd learned anything from his divorce, it was that keeping feelings bottled up inside was no use to anyone.

His instinct was to go to her. Pull her into his arms. Tell her he'd do everything in his power to make this bad situation right. But something about the way she was looking at him confirmed his fears rather than allayed them.

She'd just found out her brother was in trouble. It was very possible he wouldn't survive. And there was nothing that would send Lulu back to that dark place she'd only just crawled out of more than losing another family member.

She hung up her phone and gave him a *What gives?* gesture.

He pocketed his phone, his brain whirring with an extensive to-do list. Normally his body and his brain kicked into a familiar routine at moments like these. Sort out staff…equipment. Decide a course of action. He'd literally attended thousands of emergencies over his career. This one shouldn't be any different.

But his thoughts kept snagging on the one unfamiliar aspect of today's emergency.

It was personal.

He braced himself. She wasn't going to like the decision he had to make.

He would work this one.

She was getting benched.

244 HAWAIIAN MEDIC TO RESCUE HIS HEART

As if she had read his mind and wanted to make sure he knew she disagreed, she jogged over to him. "I'll head over to the site now."

"No." He shook his head. "You won't. Not on this one."

"You need me."

"I need you safe."

"I work safe."

Against his better judgment he huffed out a humorless, solitary, "Ha."

She went still. Too still. Her eyes were glued to him with a laser-sharp focus that seared right through to his heart. She knew why he'd made the call, but she didn't like it.

Not. One. Bit.

He was about to ask her to look after Harry, knowing she would definitely need something to do, but stopped himself short. Mixing personal and professional on a day like this was a very bad idea.

He gestured to indicate that he'd be with her in a minute, then asked his parents if they could look after Harry for a bit—preferably at their condo, which was inland and on a slightly higher elevation. A tsunami wasn't likely, but he'd hate to assure them that the beach house was safe. His dad agreed, as Zach had known he would, but his response was drowned out in a coughing fit.

Zach helped him regain his breath as yet another weight lodged in his chest. Relying on them for childcare was something he was going to have to reassess. He'd leaned on them big-time when his marriage had fallen apart, but he couldn't ignore the fact that his parents wouldn't be around forever.

His phone buzzed again. A pressing reminder that timing was critical.

"So." Lulu had her arms crossed over her chest. "Not even good enough to look after Harry anymore, am I?"

"Lulu—" There was a note of warning in his voice even he didn't like to hear. "This is for your safety."

"Is it?" she asked, and then, as she turned to walk away, she threw another question over her shoulder. "Or is it for yours?"

Unexpectedly, she wheeled on him, and a blaze of energy hit him straight in the solar plexus.

"You will not keep me from this rescue. That's my *brother* we're talking about."

"I know." He hated himself for resorting to his *Now, let's be reasonable* voice, but it was the first tool in his arsenal, so he grabbed it—because time was of the essence. The longer this played out, the less likely it was they'd find Duke. He held out his hands between them. "Lulu, you know that's not how this works. Just like surgeons, rescue crews don't go into delicate situations when it's personal."

"They're *all* personal," she bit out.

The words hit him like bullets. "Don't you think I know that?" he demanded. "Why the hell do you think I do this?"

"I don't know, Zach." She crossed her arms over her chest. "To lord it over other people? Show them how great you are? Be the big hero? It's what you do, isn't it? Show everyone that you're Mr. Perfect?"

Everything in him stilled. This wasn't how she really felt. Couldn't be. She'd been curled up in his arms this morning, all warm and cuddly, a smile on her sleeping face. When she'd woken and seen him there, his head beside hers on the pillow, her smile had doubled. She'd grinned, and whispered, "Wow. Dreams really do come true."

And now he was a self-aggrandizing hero?

He wanted to shout at her. Shake some common sense back into her. Remind her that this wasn't about her. Or her brother. Or trying to prove to the universe that she could've saved her parents if only her brothers hadn't held her back from the sea.

This was a bad thing that was happening. And it was his job to send in the best people to make it better.

"This is the right thing to do, Lulu, and you know it."

She dug her heels in. "Don't keep me off this job, Zach."

He did the same. She'd pissed him off and he felt emotion blaze up in him like flames. "You know I have to. It's how this works. How the job works."

"Well, then, why don't you take your job and shove it?" she spat back.

"What?"

"You heard me. I quit."

She shifted her weight to her other hip, her expression flickering between rage and something else. Shock at what had just come out of her mouth.

"Lulu, you love this job."

"Not if you hog-tie me and won't let me do it."

"What the hell...? Don't be like this. You know it's out of my hands."

"I know you're the boss and what you say goes. And right now I don't like what you're saying."

She was out of line, and she knew it, but what scared him was that she didn't seem to care. Her defiant expression shot him back to the first day they'd met, when his gut had told him one thing: *This girl's nothing but trouble.*

He was wishing like hell he'd listened to his gut.

He'd known there'd be hurdles in their way when they crossed the line from professional to personal. But now they were tripping him up on a level he hadn't seen coming. What if the same thing happened with Harry? What if she were to round on his boy the way she was now, fighting something she knew was the right decision?

And just like that the slim thread that had been holding his heart in place snapped. He leaned into her. Close. Real close. So no one would hear but her. "I trusted you," he said. "I trusted you more than I've ever trusted anyone since—"

He stopped himself. He wasn't going to give Lulu the satisfaction of hearing his voice crack. Screw that. If one by-the-book move was all it took to make her turn and run he and Harry didn't need her in their lives. Not now. Not ever. Lesson learned.

He pressed himself up to his full height, his voice more arctic than he'd ever heard it. "Have your resignation on my desk by the time I get back."

And then he turned and walked away.

CHAPTER TWELVE

LULU SWERVED ROUND the corner toward the EMT headquarters, narrowly missing a camper van as it trundled past in the other direction. Her heart jackhammered against her rib cage. That had been close. Too close.

An increasingly uncomfortable niggle wormed its way through to her conscience. Zach had been right to pull her off the job. She was too strung out, too frenetic, too *frightened* to work properly. But she couldn't stand by and do nothing.

She'd been too young to help when her mother had paddled out to sea, shortly followed by her father. Too inexperienced, ill-equipped, emotional. But they'd had to physically hold her down to keep her from throwing herself in and following them.

"Needle in a haystack," she'd heard one of the rescue guys say to another when the rescue boats had eventually returned, with no celebratory horn-honking to convey a success.

Needle in a haystack.

Today's rescue wasn't going to be that different. Mud was standing in for the ocean. With the same power to kill. To absorb a human— her brother—into the earth as if he hadn't existed at all.

She yanked her car into the EMT personnel parking lot, swearing under her breath when, once again, her lack of focus caused her to nearly end up bumper to bumper with an oncoming vehicle.

She grabbed her uniform from the back seat of her Jeep and ran into the office. Chen, one of Duke's high school football buddies, was on duty. When he glanced up from the call he'd just finished, he looked about as grim as she felt.

Before she could utter a word, he put up his hands. "No."

"What do you mean, no?" she bridled. "I haven't even asked you anything yet."

"Lulu. You've got a freaking uniform on your shoulder and a *Send me into the deep end* expression on your face. Not going to happen. They've got rescue crews in place and they're doing everything they can."

"*'They'* don't have me."

He mimicked her air quotes. "And *'they'* are all highly qualified rescue staff."

"They're not me."

"And they shouldn't be. You know the rules."

She wanted to scream. Kick something. She closed her eyes, regrouped and forced her voice to remain steady when she opened them again. "I know when there's a big accident it's all hands on deck. No matter what's going on."

It hadn't just been Duke and the stuntwoman riding a quad bike who'd been involved in the accident. There'd been the film crew and their support teams, too. Not everyone would've taken the fall Duke had, but there were some twenty-odd people fighting for their lives in one way or another and she wanted to be there. Helping.

"Not today, Lulu." He stood up and crossed to her.

She took a step back, needing to keep the space between them. He wasn't threatening her. He was coming in for a hug. But she didn't want it. Didn't deserve it.

Zach had been right.

She wasn't any good to anyone right now, and he'd been between an enormous rock and an immovable hard place. The best, the kindest thing she could have done was to have accepted what he'd said and let him do his job.

Even though it had been a good twenty minutes since she'd torn out of his driveway and down the coastal highway into Honolulu, she was still feeling Zach's presence as if he was right there in front of her. She could almost smell him in her nostrils. Barbecue smoke, pineapple and little boy. She could feel him in her space, leaning in close, his face taut with disbelief and unspilled anger, barely speaking above a whisper as he'd breathed out his admonishment. *I trusted you.*

She'd crossed the line. Gone way too far. Her age-old fears had roared up and superseded everything else. She'd crushed everything they'd been building into the ground as if it had never mattered at all. Which, of course, was the complete opposite of how she really felt.

She loved him. She loved Harry. The huge vacuum their absence would create in her heart was an acute reminder that the only people she had ever been able to treat this recklessly and still expect to be loved were her family.

But she'd just learned the hard way that you

couldn't be reckless with a fragile heart like Zach's. It bordered on cruel.

If the shoe had been on the other foot she would've grounded Zach, too. Would've kept him away from her kid. She probably would've given him something to do...something to make him feel useful...but sometimes—like that day she'd stood on the shore, waiting and waiting for her parents to return—the only thing you could do was pray.

Her phone had been buzzing and pinging with messages from her brothers, but the truth was she'd been too frightened to look. Too terrified to hear the news if it was bad. Which—again— confirmed that Zach's decision was the right one. She wasn't in the right headspace to be dangling from a helicopter or clawing through a mudslide without compromising her own life and possibly the lives of others. Zach had been doing what he always did. Looking out for her.

She gave her shoulders a shake and then asked the EMT dispatcher, "Have you heard anything about him? About Duke?"

The fact he was on the island at all was rare. They'd made plans to meet up now he'd got back from a film set somewhere in Africa, but had yet to make good on it. She cursed herself for not having made it a priority.

He'd always been one of her favorite big brothers, but perhaps that was because he was the one she knew the least. He was ten years older and rarely on the island, because his work took him round the world doing stunt work for some of the world's most famous action stars. Her memories of him were mostly from when she'd been a little kid. She'd always thought of him as the fun one. The one who'd throw her on his back and run her round the backyard, neighing and whinnying like he was a horse, when she'd gone through her *I want a pony* phase. The fact he'd become a stuntman had been a surprise to no one. Tall, muscular and fearless, he was every action film director's dream come true.

She couldn't begin to imagine a world that didn't have all that energy in it.

She felt her face muscles twitch as reality hit. No matter who she went to, how many favors she tried to beg, she was going to hit wall after wall after wall. The only thing she could do was what the rest of her family was doing. Wait for news.

She found Makoa and Pekelo at her grandmother's house. The three of them were staring blankly at tall glasses of iced tea, ice cubes long melted. Her grandmother filled her in. Laird was on a flight over from Maui and Kili, the navy SEAL, was being kept updated by his admiral on the aircraft carrier he was posted on somewhere on the other side of the world.

"Where's your boyfriend?" Mak asked.

What little composure Lulu had left crumpled.

"Hey!" Her brother was up and by her side in an instant. "What'd he do to you? Want us to run him back to the mainland? He's still on probation, right?"

"No, it's nothing like that. It's me. I'm the one who messed up," Lulu said, tears finally surfacing and trickling down her cheeks.

"What'd you do?"

"I quit. I quit my job." She could barely believe she'd been such a stupid idiot.

"Why?" Pekelo asked.

"He grounded me."

Mak snorted in disbelief. "Lulu, you got problems."

"Yeah? Tell me about it, Mr. Perfect!" she snapped.

He rapped his knuckles on the table, commanding their attention. "It's how it works, Mini.

You don't get to pick and choose which rules to follow. They exist to keep us alive, yeah? You think I want to be here when I know I'd be more helpful up there? I won those search and rescue games for a reason. I'm the best there is. And they've grounded me. If I didn't know in my heart that those rules are right I'd be up on that hillside trying to dig my brother out with my bare hands!"

Lulu nodded and buried her head in her hands, ashamed of having taken Zach's decision so personally. And, yes, of course she knew exactly what Mak was talking about. She'd be doing exactly the same if she was allowed. They all would. But instead they were having to find the same faith the general public placed in them when they set out to rescue their loved ones.

I trusted you.

The words played on a loop in her mind, over and over, grating against all the other decisions she should have made.

How on earth was she going to fix this?

When she looked up, Makoa was waiting for her, expectant. "What's really going on, Mini?"

It was a good question. One that had got so tangled up in the melee she hardly remembered where all her churned up feelings had begun. And then, clear as a bell, she remembered Casey, sitting on that picnic table, as casual as could be, wondering aloud when Lulu would leave Zach.

Her stomach turned as she realized just how beautifully Casey had put a name to her predictability. How it had proved true so quickly. It had taken…what? Two minutes? Three? A tiny earthquake had cracked her world in two. One decision that she knew Zach had struggled to take and she'd snapped like a twig. She'd taken everything she felt for him and his son and shoved it in his face as if they meant nothing to her.

"I messed up," she finally admitted.

Makoa pulled another chair up to the table they were all gathered round and had her sit down. She poured her heart out to them. Told them everything. How she'd not been sure about Zach at first, how they'd seemed to clash so much, but how, eventually, she'd seen how similar they both were. She told them how they'd been fighting off deeply embedded fears and overcoming them. Together. And then she'd gone and ruined it all when she'd wanted to fix something she never could.

No matter how many rescues she went on, her

parents would never, ever come back. She saw that now. Saw the futility of her misplaced anger. The destructiveness it had wrought in her life. Never enabling her to establish deep, enduring friendships or relationships until…until she'd gone and done it with the single most wonderful man she'd ever met. Zach Murphy.

Her grandmother, who had sat silently throughout her emotional outpouring, took a long drink of her tea, then said, "'A humble person walks carefully so as not to hurt others.'"

"I think I already messed that part up, Gran," Lulu said miserably. "Got any other sayings that might help me out of this mess?"

Her grandmother's lips softened and twitched lightly into a smile. "Quite a few."

"Lay 'em on me. All of them."

Her grandmother gave them each a thoughtful inspection. When her eyes landed on Lulu she said, "'A child behaves like those who reared her.'"

Lulu and her brothers sat up at that. "What do you mean?" she asked.

"You're all headstrong! Tempestuous. Too quick to decide upon a solution to a problem."

Lulu huffed out a dark laugh. "Jeez, Gran. Kick a girl when she's down, why don't you?"

Makoa gave her a light fist bump, but because they all loved and respected their grandmother they fell silent as she cleared her throat to continue.

"There's another side to those traits all of you possess. Bravery. Strength. Wisdom. Especially you, Lulu. But it's up to you which traits you most want the world to see."

The comment landed where it had been meant to. In her heart.

She knew now, beyond a shadow of a doubt, that she loved Zach. She would eat a thousand humble pies—more, if it would fix what had happened between them. He had a son he cared for more than himself. He knew exactly what sacrifice was. What trust was. And she'd all but spat on the trust she knew he held sacred.

She wasn't sure he would ever forgive her for it. But she had to find out. And there was only one way to go about it.

Earn both his forgiveness and his trust.

"I've got to go." She gave her brothers each a hug, and her grandmother an extralong one. "Thanks, Gran. Wish me luck."

Her grandmother pulled back, her arms still around her, and smiled. "You don't need luck, child. You need to do what you've taken a lifetime to realize."

"Which is?"

"Look to the future. It is the only way to make peace with the past."

And in that instant Lulu suddenly understood how her grandmother was able to have such a Zen-like relationship with life. She'd been as hollowed out by grief as the rest of them when Lulu's parents had died. But she'd had six grandchildren to help raise, their futures to think about. Being consumed by the pain of loss would never have helped anything or anyone.

Lulu had fallen victim to exactly that. Pinning the urgency of each and every rescue to some sort of scorecard she'd made with the universe. If, one day, she got enough points, she'd get the top job at work and her dream house. Neither of which would mean anything without Zach and Harry by her side.

She gave her gran's cheek a kiss, then said, "I'll meet you all at the hospital in a bit."

Mak frowned at her. "What are you talking about?"

"Duke's going to need us there. Whether he's in surgery or just suffering from a bruised ego. And we'll be there for him."

Pek frowned, and started to say something, but she cut him off. "If Duke's not there...we'll be there for everyone else. Yeah? Like he'd want us to be."

Their frowns turned into soft smiles and nods of affirmation.

She held up her phone. "Keep in touch, yeah? I've got to put a few things right."

"Are you going to answer it this time?" asked Mak.

"Every time," she said, meaning it.

She wouldn't ignore her family, her friends—the people who loved her most—anymore. It was time to become the woman she'd always wanted to be. A good one.

CHAPTER THIRTEEN

THE LANDSLIDE WAS BAD. Real bad.

The only way the two of them would've stood a chance of surviving was to have been thrown beyond the crush of iron soil, rock and tree roots.

The helicopter was doing its best to navigate the ravine, where any survivors would be found.

"Lower," Zach instructed as he eagle-eyed the sun glinting off a bit of silver. He was sure he could see it now. The handlebar of a quad bike. "A couple more meters, Stew."

Stewart's voice crackled through his earpiece. "That's as far as I can get the chopper down, Zach. You're either going to have unclip and risk having to hike out, or we need to find somewhere else to put you down."

He thought of Lulu's face. The way it had drained of blood as she'd heard the news about her brother. The way tears had poured down her cheeks as she had performed CPR on the "dead" mannequin back when they'd been in the search and rescue games. She didn't give up. Not until she had to. And he was a long way from having to.

"I'll unclip."

"Is that wise?"

No. It wasn't. But there weren't an awful lot of rational thoughts going through his head right now. What he should've done was taken himself off the job, too, but right now he needed work like he needed oxygen. It was his go-to coping mechanism—slapping the blinkers on, closing off the rest of the world, so that his brain had a chance to absorb whatever the hell it was that had happened and do something positive. Something helpful.

Guilt pierced through his focus.

Exactly like Lulu.

If she wasn't helping, all her demons swarmed in. And he'd left her there on her own, with nothing but her fears and a demand for her resignation as companions.

As he unclipped the stretcher, and then himself, dropping to his knees for a body roll to take the impact of the fall, realization dawned. This was his pattern. If he screwed something up he had to go fix something else. Anything but the actual problem. When his dad had got sick after 9/11 he'd retrained as a medic. When his son had been born with a disability he'd started running marathons for the cerebral palsy charity instead of spending time where he should have. In his marriage.

Cause and effect. Cause and effect.

He'd fallen in love with Lulu. It had scared the hell out of him—not having control over her, not being able to predict her next move. Or, more to the point, keep her safe.

He'd cornered her into quitting. Forced her hand when he knew better than anyone that being handed a shovel and told to dig would've been a kinder, more loving thing to do.

But he'd seen red and walked away. Had wanted control of a situation he had no capacity or right to control.

Letting his wife go had been the safest option for his son.

Letting Lulu go…

Every pore in his body was telling him it had been the wrong decision. A cowardly way of making her take the fall for a situation that scared the hell out of him. Loving someone who knew her own mind. Her strengths. Her weaknesses. And his.

She'd read him like a book and when he'd shown her his true colors, his fears masked as machismo, she hadn't wanted any part of it. He didn't blame her.

He felt the ground shift beneath his feet as he tried to stand. There were tens of thousands of tons of earth here. Displaced soil and rock from the cliff… And one handlebar from a quad bike.

He shot off a flare gun, hoping the fire and rescue crew hiking in from the coast would see it through the jungle canopy, then dropped to his knees, pulled his collapsible spade from his backpack and began to dig.

A few minutes later the ground crew arrived. Perimeters were marked out. Trajectories calculated for how far Duke and the other quad rider—a stuntwoman called Jessica—would've been thrown. They dug and dug and dug as if their lives depended upon it. Theirs might not, but Duke's and Jessica's did.

A shout went up. They'd found Duke.

Zach was by his side in an instant. He'd unearthed more than his fair share of survivors from collapsed structures and the odd sinkhole.

He knew one false move could make the difference between life and death.

With infinite care, they unearthed him, relief flooding through the group like the sun coming out from behind a storm cloud when they discovered he was alive. He'd obviously sustained some internal injuries—that was made apparent by his low, thready pulse—but the fact he'd been wearing a helmet had played a massive role in his survival. From the angle of one of his legs, there would be at least one compound fracture to tend to as well.

After carefully securing him to the stretcher, Zach put a neck brace on him, checked for any outward signs of bleeding or additional compound fractures that needed immediate attention, and then, fairly certain that the only thing holding him together was his cleverly designed costume—a padded motorcycle suit sewn into a business suit—left him intact.

Zach radioed Stewart, asking him to try to get the cables down one last time before they made the decision to walk him out. The half hour or so it would take to carry him to the nearest road was time that might mean the difference between life and death. And there was no way Zach was going to tell Lulu they hadn't done everything humanly possible to ensure the outcome they all wanted.

It took Stewart a minute or two longer than it normally would have, but he did it. Zach clipped himself to the safety basket and rode up with Duke, telling him over and over how much his family was looking forward to seeing him again…how much they cared…how he should hang on because help was close at hand.

When they landed on the roof of the hospital, emergency medical staff were there to take over, but Zach ran in with them, anyway.

"You can't come in, man," said one of the doctors, his eyes on Zach's dirt-covered uniform. "Operating room has to stay sterile."

Zach backed off, the swinging doors of the OR practically hitting him in the face. He felt his phone vibrate. He grabbed it out of his safety vest. Twenty messages were sitting there. The phone buzzed again. Twenty-one. All of them from Lulu.

She was here. In the hospital. He wasn't to worry, but—

He jammed the phone in his pocket and took off for the emergency room entrance at a run, heart pounding, brain buzzing with too many possibilities—all of them dark—to let just one take purchase.

He scanned the busy waiting room. He saw Harry first, and then Lulu. They were playing a board game on a little table in the children's play area. Lulu was keeping Harry actively engaged while sending yet another text under the table out of Harry's eye line.

Zach didn't know what he felt. Relief. Gratitude. Fear. They weren't here for the fun of it.

"Duke's in surgery," he said.

"Your dad's had a heart attack," Lulu said at the same time.

"He's going to make it." They spoke simultaneously. Then again. "You go."

Nervous laughter filled the space between them until Zach gestured for her to speak.

"Your dad had a heart attack. He's alive. I got some aspirin into him straight away, which helped. He's getting a couple of stents put in, but other than that he should be good as new. Your mom's with him now."

Harry grabbed his dad in a waist-high hug and beamed up at him. "Lulu saved Grandpa!"

Zach shook his head, not understanding. "Were you in the ambulance?"

"No. I was over at your parents'."

He gave her a blank look.

She lowered her voice, giving Harry's head a little scrub. "I owed this little man an apology for running out on him. And your parents. And you." She winced and gave an apologetic smile. "I might've said a few things I didn't mean..."

"You had every right. I was thinking more like an overprotective boyfriend than a boss."

She opened her mouth and goldfished, a sheen of emotion glossing her eyes.

"Don't cry, Lulu!" Harry dug into his pocket and handed her a tissue.

She thanked him and looked across at Zach, as though she wanted to say something but couldn't.

Harry jumped in and explained how Lulu had come over and apologized to them all for leaving the barbecue. "She said she was scared for her brother, and needed to see her family, but that made her realize she felt like *we* were family, too! She said she loved you, Daddy. That you made her a better person." He started singing a little song, the lyrics composed of three words. "Lulu loves Daddy... Lulu loves Daddy..."

Their eyes met, and the connection was so strong between them that Zach felt as if she had actually handed him her heart.

Lulu still loved him.

Harry tugged his hand, keen to finish his story. "And then Grandma and Grandpa were so happy they said we better have ice cream. So Grandpa went to the freezer, but he fell down, and Lulu pressed on his chest until the ambulance came, and now he's okay."

Again his eyes snapped to hers. "You did CPR on my dad?"

She nodded. "And you dug my brother out of a mountain."

And there it was. Love in a nutshell. You did whatever you had to do, whether or not you knew that your love was going to be returned.

A not entirely settled peace surrounded them. They both had questions. Lots of them.

They started with facts.

He filled her in on how they'd found Duke and the injuries he thought he had. "I suspect he'll need quite a bit of recovery time, and a lot of physio, but from the looks of this waiting room he's got a pretty amazing support team."

They both looked round and saw that the room

had filled up. It was so full, friends were actually having to wait outside as well as in.

"Thank you," she said, her voice scratchy with emotion. "You went above and beyond. If you hadn't pushed things..." she took a wavery breath "...he might not have a recovery to fight through."

Zach shook his head. "I did what I had to."

"You did more than that," she replied, with a fierceness that warmed him straight through to his heart. "I have it on good authority that you stepped outside the rule book to find him."

"What? How?"

Lulu pointed over to another section of the waiting room—one that was filled to the gunnels with tall, muscular, dark-haired men in various uniforms. Her brothers and their in-laws, and their brothers, and everyone else she'd grown up with. There in the middle of them was Makoa, who gave her a little flick of the chin to say he saw what was going on.

A gathering like this a year ago—hell, a month ago—would've sent her running for the ocean, surfboard tucked under her arm, ready to paddle out as far and as fast as she could. Doubly so if they'd caught her baring her heart to someone right here in the middle of it all.

But she'd learned something today. Protectiveness didn't have to mean suffocation. It could mean support. Something to hold all the emotions she felt in balance, catching her as she negotiated the best course of action. Sometimes she'd be right. Sometimes she'd be wrong.

She'd been wrong to think Zach was trying to sideline her.

She'd been right to find his parents and Harry, even not knowing if Zach would speak with her again.

When Harry saw where Lulu was looking, he waved at Mak. Her brother grinned at the little boy, his hand instantly folding into the island greeting. Harry jumped up and down, thrilled to have someone so spectacular singling him out for a *shaka*.

Mak, clearly sensing that Lulu and Zach were having an important talk, beckoned the little boy over.

"You cool with that?" Lulu asked, hanging on to the hood of Harry's hoodie so that he wouldn't run off.

"Of course," Zach said. "I know he'll be safe."

It was his version of saying that he trusted her and her family, and it meant the world. He might as well have got down on bended knee and asked her to spend the rest of his life with her. Told her he loved her. But they weren't there just yet.

Lulu gave Mak a wave of thanks when she saw him pick the boy up and start introducing him to everyone as Harry the Beast, well aware that a six-year-old around a sea of supersize men would be a lot to handle.

Mahalo, she mouthed to her brother, and then to Zach she said, "I heard Duke was coming in from Casey. I was already here with your dad, so I let these guys know. They wanted to be here in case—you know—in case it hadn't gone according to plan..." She continued in a rush. "Everyone's gathered here now, and they will head out to help the crews who are looking for Jessica." Her eyes flicked to the waiting room clock. "Only a couple more hours until sunset."

She looked up at him. His blue eyes were filled with the love she'd been so frightened of receiving. The love she had to put through one more test.

"If it's cool with you, I'm going to help."

Zach pulled her to him and tipped his head

to hers. "I shouldn't have stopped you before. It wasn't my place."

"No," she corrected. "You were right. I was out of my mind. I needed the proverbial slap in the face."

He flinched and pulled back at her choice of words.

She held up her hands. "I know you weren't doing what you did to hurt me. Quite the opposite."

He nodded. "I've got to go see my dad—but, Lulu, we need to talk. Properly."

"I know. We will. For as long as we need to. Days, if necessary. Which reminds me..." She dug in her pocket for a piece of paper. "I have to give you this."

He knew what it was without looking at it. "No. I won't accept it."

"You have to."

"No, I don't."

She gave a gentle laugh, her features softening with affection. "You made me realize something really important today."

"What? That you hated your boss?"

"No. That I really, genuinely, do not want that job anymore."

"What? You love it."

"I do…but I love giving back more."

He shook his head, clearly not understanding.

"I want to work for Superstars Surf Club. Full-time."

"I don't understand… I thought Chantal was the only paid staff member."

"She was," Lulu said. "Until she got an offer to set up another Superstars Surf Club in Australia."

Zach let out a low whistle. "That sounds like an offer that would be hard to say no to." His brow creased. "How did you fit all these things into an afternoon? Visiting your family, my family, saving my dad's life, writing a resignation letter and finding a new job?"

She gave him a sheepish smile. "I can do a lot when I put my mind to it."

His smile was soft and sincere, infused with the deep kindness she'd first spotted in him back when she'd thought he was someone who would make her life hell. Meeting him hadn't been hell, but she felt as though she'd been through a journey. One of those epic, life-changing ones that had taken her heart and mind and plunged her deep into the parts of her life she'd been actively ignoring.

Falling in love with Zach had meant confronting demons and, to her disbelief, she had come out whole. Better than whole. She was in love, and she couldn't wait to spend a lifetime of sharing this amazing feeling with Zach and Harry.

He ran a couple of fingers through her hair, tucking it back behind her ear. "I love you, Lulu Kahale. You're mad as a hatter, but you're good for me. You remind me that being a better person doesn't always mean sticking to the rule book."

"I love you, too. And Harry," she added, wanting him to know that she knew they came as a package deal. She went up on tiptoe and gave him a kiss. "Go see your dad. I'll meet you in a few hours, yeah?"

He returned the kiss, and the depth of connection they'd just shared was transferred between them like energy. She'd never do anything again to compromise what they had together. No matter what.

"*Mahalo*, Zach."

"Thank you? For what?"

"For being you. For taking a chance on me."

"There was no chance in this, my love," Zach

said, cupping her cheeks with his hands. "This was destiny. And don't you forget it."

She wouldn't. She wouldn't ever forget. Not as long as she had a heart beating in her chest.

EPILOGUE

One year later

LULU HID BEHIND a palm tree, watching as everyone filtered down onto the beach, where there were huge plank benches spread in a massive circle. And her grandmother, her brothers—Duke walking without his cane for the first time in a year.

They were all so different from the people they'd been just one year ago.

Duke had ended up needing months of recovery in the hospital. His injuries had been far more profound than they'd originally thought. He'd spent those long months not only diligently following his strict rehab routine, but coming up with new safety guidelines for stuntmen and women.

Today he was pushing Jessica in her new wheelchair, sportier than the one she'd initially had after her injuries had made it clear she wouldn't walk again. But she swam. Every day with her rehab specialist in the pool, and twice a week with Lulu in the ocean, on a surfboard kitted out with special support harnesses.

Makoa was wearing a traditional outfit, of course. As were her grandmother and her brother Laird. Kili was wearing his Navy dress whites uniform and looking stupidly handsome, even if he was her brother. And Pekelo was wearing one of his trademark Hawaiian sunset shirts... the goof.

All of them were wearing leis. All of them except for Lulu, who was wearing a crown of flowers because today, of all of the days in her life, she truly felt like Hawaiian royalty.

Harry had insisted upon wearing a traditional Hawaiian shirt, covered in flowers and surfboards. Zach was wearing a gorgeous linen suit that, if possible, made him look even more gorgeous than he'd been that first day, when she'd seen him and thought, *Uh-oh, here we go... Fire and ice don't mix.*

But it turned out they did when they worked together. Lived together. Loved together.

When most of the guests had arrived, Mak pulled out the family's conch shell horn and sounded several long calls—the Hawaiian way of calling the gathering together and bringing everyone they'd asked to join them into the same mind space—into the beautiful reflective energy that was charged with the power of bringing Zach and Lulu together as husband and wife.

As the reverend began to chant the *Oli Aloha*, Lulu began her journey down the "aisle" to the center of the circle, where Zach stood. They'd agreed together that they wanted a circle. A shared space for friends and family to witness their public declaration of shared love. A reminder that once they were joined together they wouldn't just be two people—or, in their case, three—but an entire community made up of family and friends. It fitted perfectly with the *Oli Aloha*'s verses, which spoke of seeking a loved one, finding them and becoming one with each other and with all who loved them.

Throughout the ceremony—complete with the exchanging of leis and the Hawaiian ring blessing—Zach and Lulu beamed at one another. They'd been through it all with the reverend several times, but this time it was as if every cell in their bodies knew it was the one that counted.

Once they had exchanged their vows, and their

hands had been bound together with a lei for a blessing that reminded them that it wasn't anything physical that bound them together, it was love, they were invited to kiss and seal the marriage.

Zach pulled her so close to him she actually felt her feet lift up and off the ground. The guests began to laugh.

"Why are they laughing?" Zach whispered against her lips. "Don't they do kissing the bride in Hawaii?"

"They do," she said, kissing him in between ever fewer words. "But normally the bride's flipflops don't fall off when the groom kisses her."

"Just like Cinderella!" He grinned.

"Better than Cinderella," she said, as the reverend asked them to face one another for the final step of the ceremony.

"Why's that?" asked Zach, reluctantly returning her to the ground, weaving his fingers through hers.

"Because Prince Charming lives in a castle and we live somewhere far, far superior."

They grinned and looked up at Turtle Hideaway, which was absolutely covered in tropical flowers and looked more as if it should be a float in an Aloha Parade than the place where they were going to spend their honeymoon.

The reverend began to recite the *He Alo A He Alo*.

Lulu beamed at Zach as the short prayer invited them to share *aloha* in their marriage.

"For those of you who do not know," said the reverend, "*Alo* means person and *ha* means breath. Together Lulu and Zach will honor the breath of life they have each been given and the added strength that comes from the love they share."

"Do we get to kiss again?" Zach asked.

"By all means. It's your life to live. Together."

And that was the joy of giving herself to Zach, Lulu thought as she willingly tucked herself into her husband's warm embrace. Giving meant receiving. Until she'd learned to give herself completely to him, without any hope or expectation of anything in return, she hadn't known the true meaning of love. And now that she had it was better than she could ever have imagined.

* * * * *

LET'S TALK
Romance

For exclusive extracts, competitions
and special offers, find us online:

 facebook.com/millsandboon

 @millsandboonuk

 @millsandboon

Or get in touch on 0844 844 1351*

For all the latest titles coming soon,
visit millsandboon.co.uk/nextmonth